Benjamin Franklin Hatch

Spiritualists' Iniquities Unmasked, and the Hatch Divorce Case

Anatiposi

Benjamin Franklin Hatch

Spiritualists' Iniquities Unmasked, and the Hatch Divorce Case

Reprint of the original, first published in 1859.

1st Edition 2023 | ISBN: 978-3-38232-812-2

Anatiposi Verlag is an imprint of Outlook Verlagsgesellschaft mbH.

Verlag (Publisher): Outlook Verlag GmbH, Zeilweg 44, 60439 Frankfurt, Deutschland
Vertretungsberechtigt (Authorized to represent): E. Roepke, Zeilweg 44, 60439 Frankfurt, Deutschland
Druck (Print): Books on Demand GmbH, In de Tarpen 42, 22848 Norderstedt, Deutschland

SPIRITUALISTS'

INIQUITIES UNMASKED,

AND

THE HATCH DIVORCE CASE.

BY

B. F. HATCH, M. D.

〰〰〰

New-York:
PUBLISHED FOR THE AUTHOR.
1859.

INTRODUCTION.

My task is an unpleasant one ; but, urged on by the irresistible power of a sense of duty, I fearlessly undertake its accomplishment. I am aware that in proportion to the magnitude of the evils which I may attack—and especially if it be in divine order, and the falsities which I expose—I shall array against myself whole societies of anarchical spirits, both in and out of the form. The vilest calumny against the author of their exposure will be thrown up as a rampart of defence, and in this way an attempt will be made to destroy the influence of truths which they cannot successfully controvert. However well they may apparently succeed for a while, it will be remembered that truth contains within itself an almighty power which will cause it, sooner or later, to spring forth through all the rubbish of falsehood and wrong which may be heaped upon it, and triumph over every opposing obstacle. With this conviction, I shall state such facts as have come under my own observation, or have been given me from such sources as are authentic, and leave the result with Him who often overrules seeming evils for the general good.

All true persons, of whatever class, will rejoice in the establishment of Good and Truth ; and the overthrow of falsehood and wrong can be mourned only by those whose inverted nature causes them, apparently, to feed with delight upon its miasmatic poison. The men and women who prefer a favored theory to the stern reality of facts, give evidence that they have not traveled far in that path which leads to true wisdom and a harmonious life. The evolutions of Truth should keep us ever active in the search of higher wisdom, and thus, step by step, hasten towards that goal to which we are all aspiring. Therefore, the stability or fixedness of opinion is no indication of either an active or a progressive mind. The discoveries of all past time come rushing upon us like the mighty ocean wave, and stimulate us to still greater exertion in the arcana of nature. It should be our aim to develop an orthodoxy which shall be both rational and cosmical, and maintain, at the same time, a liberality both humane and catholic. This would afford a resting place and a centre of reconciliation where Christian men of all persuasions may unite in a convergent harmony of doctrine, and thus free themselves from misconception of what belongs to a rational philosophy, and enable them to establish inmost heart-relations with each other.

I am not unaware that too frequently we make enemies of those whom, with the greatest diligence, we seek to bless. The pointing out of errors, and the reproof of faults is not a pleasing task. In this respect the motive which stimulates to the most charitable act is liable to be misinterpreted, and the most beneficent rebuke transformed into malignant slander. The feeling in all is strong for approbation, and he who tells another his faults is not believed to be a friend. If what I have to say shall have no effect upon those whose wills are now held in vassalage, it may prevent many others from becoming the victims of a like condition. The rational should take warning by the condition of those who are already subjugated to an infernal influence, over which they have ceased to have control. Those who yield their individuality to the dictation of others, will, sooner or later, reap a prolific harvest of regret and sorrow. Prosperity may for awhile appear to be the result, for

" Whom the gods would destroy, they first make mad."

Nine years of investigation and observation have not left me wholly unacquainted with the facts, philosophy and practical workings of Spiritualism ; and if I present this to an intelligent public, I trust that it may, at least, do me the justice to attribute it to a sense of duty, rather than any feelings of vindictiveness towards a class of people with whom I have been so long identified. So earnestly have I been engaged hitherto in establishing a belief in the phenomena, that to a great extent I overlooked its moral, social and religious bearings.

A few months of leisure has afforded me an opportunity of reviewing the past, criticising the Spiritualists' theory and observing their results. Many of their theories are founded in the wildest delusion, their results most direful, as will be plainly seen as we proceed. In saying what I feel that I must, a few will most heartily approve, many condemn. I am not unaware that I shall bring down upon myself the most bitter vituperation and slander without measure. I once honestly believed that there would be much general good result from the opening of the avenues of spiritual intercourse ; therefore, I was active in its promulgation. The question is frequently asked, if my domestic afflictions was not the cause of the change of my opinion ? Her sudden transition, and that in so brief an absence, led me to investigate the cause, and I soon learnt that her condition was the inevitable result of all mental spiritual control. It was the antidote which awakened me from the stupor of an infernal philosophy and brought me to my senses. I recognize no Spiritualism which is in contradistinction to the revelations of Heaven. Though I once threw Christianity overboard, I thank God that I have again been made its recipient.

The believers in spiritual intercourse can now be numbered by millions, and embrace all classes of society among its votaries. Whether their faith has any basis in truth, or is the mere working of overwrought imagination, it becomes a theme worthy of candid consideration and close criticism. There are various opinions of its utility or its practical workings upon society. The extensive opportunity which I have had, and that too among the first-class of Spiritualists, of learning its nature and results, I think will enable me to lay just claims to being a competent witness in the matter.

I am aware that what I have to say will offend many who are less acquainted with the whole phenomena than myself, and such as may feel themselves involved, and will please others ; but it is for neither purpose that I write, but that the inexperienced may more fully comprehend the dangers attending it. I am frequently asked if I still believe in the phenomena of Spiritualism. I answer, Yes. I should deem it more than a waste of time to write about what does not exist. Spiritualism in all its physical facts is true ; but through it all, there is a powerful influx of an infernal auror into nearly all mediumistic minds, which greatly corrupts the moral sensibility, and proves, almost universally, terribly disastrous to its victims.

I have heard much of the improvement of individuals in consequence of a belief in Spiritualism. With such I have had no acquaintance. But I have known many whose integrity of character and uprightness of purpose rendered them worthy examples to all around, but who, on becoming mediums, and giving up their individuality, also gave up every sense of honor and decency. A less degree of severity in this remark will apply to a large class of both mediums and believers. There are thousands of high minded and intelligent Spiritualists who will agree with me that it is no slander in saying, that the inculcation of no doctrine in this country has ever shown such disastrous moral and social results as the spiritual theories. Like an all-destructive miasma, which almost imperceptibly poisons the soul, it has made victims of tens of thousands of its votaries, and secretly crept into many other avenues of society, until it is almost popularizing those social conditions which every good citizen must most deeply deplore. Iniquities which have justly received the condemnation of centuries are openly upheld ; vices which would destroy every wholesome regulation of society are crowned as virtues ; prostitution is believed to be fidelity to self ; marriage an outrage on freedom ; love evanescent, and, like the bee, should sip the sweets wherever found ; bastards are claimed to be spiritually begotten. All change, of whatever nature, is believed to be an improvement, as there is no retrogression. Iniquity is only the effervescence of the outworkings of a heavenly destiny. God is shorn of his personality, and becomes simply a permeating principle, the Bible a libel on common sense, and Christ a mere medium, hardly equal to the spiritual babies of " this more progressive age."

With such doctrines before us, what have we to hope ? That they are rapidly increasing no one can deny. The end is not yet. One thing is favorable : many of the more upright and intelligent among them are beginning to see this condition of things, and are setting their faces against it. But they are the exceptions, and not the rule. A blind infatuation appears to drive them headlong into the whirlpool of passion, and in their wild delirium they mistake and fondly read upon their banner damnation for " liberty."

I publish this work from a full conviction of its requirments. It is not pleasant to speak of the faults of others, or parade my own troubles before the world. I will do neither, farther than is necessary to illustrate the general principle contained in the following pages. I am striking at an *evil*, not individuals, and shall use individuals only to demonstrate what I say. My letters in the New York papers have been, by many, pronounced declamatory, and not sufficiently specific—such shall not be the fault with this. With the scalpel of truth, I shall freely open the abcesses of social and moral corruption ; and the caustic will be applied, not to destroy, but to cleanse. Evils to be remedied must be freely exposed and discouraged, and if I succeed in awaking public attention to this hydra-headed monster, which is now coiling its slimy folds in the bosom of humanity, and thus cause him to be cast out, as Jesus cast out devils of old ; in other words, if I succeed in effectually warning the people against the most deceitful and damning of all infatuations which ever infested the earth, my object will be accomplished.

B. F. HATCH, M.D

New York, April, 1859.

SOCIAL AND MORAL BEARINGS OF MEDIUMSHIP.

The greatest number of Spiritualists of this country are those who simply believe in the phenomena, but who have paid but little or no attention to its theories or practical workings. It, therefore, has but little or no influence upon them, their morals and position remaining unchanged ; and it is from the influence of this class that it has been able so long to maintain its position in society. Therefore, it has depended upon its mere nominal believers to give it character and not upon its real votaries. This is a fact which has not hitherto been duly considered. Such being the case, we shall be obliged to pass by all these, denying their being true representatives of Spiritualism, and come directly to its public advocates and real votaries—such as make it their religion. No one has ever pretended to claim that a mere belief in the facts of spiritual intercourse, at once, wholly transforms a long and well regulated life ; and those who hang upon the skirts of its new-made converts for character, only virtually acknowledge that their intercourse with spirits has added nothing to their own morals. If it be a religion sent of God, we should have a right to expect that its oldest believers and most ardent and practical admirers, would shine forth as its brightest moral lights. But just the reverse is the case. And the instances which I shall point out to prove the depravity of Spiritualism, will be those who have been engaged in it from the commencement, and who started with high moral and social positions. I, therefore, cannot be accused of bringing examples which it has failed to reform, and which may be found in any class of society, but those it has actually *degraded*— such as once truly enjoyed honorable positions, but can now lay no just claim to public confidence. If, in this way, the fact is substantiated that Spiritualism is subversive of public morals and virtue, just in proportion to the extent of an adherance to its doctrines, then its evil tendency is clearly sustained, and the well intentioned everywhere should set their face against it.

The charge has been brought against me, in my exposition of Spiritualism, that I unreasonably expected a perfect reform of all the wayward ones who became interested in its phenomena. I repel this charge by saying that I do not ask for proof of a reform of any one ; but only that it does not *degrade and ruin* nearly all who yield themselves up to its influence. If I can prove that it is pregnant with *positive evil*, without bringing forth any *real good*, then my position becomes fully sustained ; and this is exactly what I intend to do.

Admitting Spiritual intercourse to be true, which I claim, the inquiry naturally arises, what is the class of Spirits which is the most nearly allied to earth, and thus the most effectually controls our mediums ? In other words, what is the character which those Spirits have claimed for themselves, which every where make the most powerful physical manifestations ? In this life they were known as pirates, thieves, robbers, murderers and wantons. Such as whose spiritual condition is yet so gross and material, that they are still able to come in direct rapport with the external world and act upon physical substances. The Spiritualists themselves claim that the most of the physical manifestations are made by this class of Spirits, and are important only as they demonstrate the phenomena. Now I am willing to grant that the physical and mental control of mediums is one grade higher than this. In other words, that they are influenced by Spirits of a more intellectual cast, but if we can judge from the results which follows, of the most depraved morals. These Spirits will inculcate such doctrines as will secure the confidence and meet the approbation of those to whom they are given. They nearly always come in the name of some near and dearly beloved kindred, or as especially appointed guardian angels. For a while, their love for us and interest in our welfare, is all that we could desire, and their promises are most faithfully kept, until our confidence is secured. And then, step by step, as we are able to receive it, they inculcate their sophistry and pervert the morals until they complete the ruin of their deluded victims. The time required to accomplish this is long or short, according to the inherent goodness, or discretion which they are obliged to overcome, but being confident of final success. Thus Spiritualists are not ruined in a day, often times requiring years ; but Spirits, to make secure their work, appeal to the strongest passions of their victims ; with many their lust, others their affections, and still others their ambition—all of which they often greatly intensify. They will personate whoever may be desired, and thus our loved ones communed through every medium, and Websters, Clays, Shakspears, Bacons, Swedenbourgs, etc., have become sufficiently numerous to be omnipresent, and their doctrines are always such as the circle requires. Thus they "become all things to all men, that they may" ruin some ; and they cannot but rejoice at their success. Sometimes they manifest themselves in their real character, and then we discover the most terrible maliciousness. Mrs. Hatch is universally acknowledged to stand as high in integrity and uprightness of purpose, as any medium in America ; and, therefore, would be likely to draw about her as elevated a class of Spirits ; nevertheless, when her controlling spirit has thrown off the mask of deception, and while she was entranced so as to be externally wholly unconscious, she has been made to threaten the entire destruction of her own conjugal happiness, and to effect her own ruin ; and that they would never leave nor forsake her until they had made her the scorn and contempt of society—that they had only permitted her short and brilliant career in order to make more perfect and awful her destruction. No epithets or language was too malicious for them (Spirits) to use ; no remonstrance or admonition would appear to have the least influence upon them ; she would be strangled until her face would turn purple, the lungs collapsed to a degree which would appear impossible, and live ; the brain so tortured that hours of the wildest delirium would follow, and when they had accomplished their present object, they would utter a ha ! ha ! ha ! as it appeared to me, would cause even the inhabitants of hell itself to shudder.

Mrs. Hatch, uninfluenced by Spirits, or unobsessed, comes the nearest my highest ideal of woman of any one I ever met on earth ; gentle, kind, loving and intellectual to a remarkable degree. But since those infernal influences have seen fit to change her course, I have stood appalled before her terrific wrath. The most unrelenting and merciless cruelty has captivated her soul, and moral consciousness is wholly lost in her vengeance. The agonies of the rack for her husband would be the most delicious music to her ears. All this mighty and wonderful change occurred in a single day. I know the extremity, but the truthfulness of this statement. Do not understand me as censuring her, for my love for, and confidence in her are limited only by the extent of my ability ; but her gentle, susceptible, ardent and yielding nature infested by demons within, and surround-

ed by those of a corresponding condition without, her own individuality is swallowed up in the vertex of evil. Upon this sad moral condition nearly all the Spiritualists fatten with delight, and those who
are most active in perpetuating it, resort to the vilest means to accomplish their object. But the facts pertaining to this will be given
in another place.

This is not a solitary case, but a representative of nearly every
mental medium in the country. I will give another example in this
city. A lady, past the middle age of life, who is not known as a
Spiritualist, and had paid no attention to the subject, was one day
unexpectedly entranced, which lasted for three days. Up to that time
her gentle, kind, and loving disposition made her the admiration of
all who knew her. But during that entrancement her whole moral
and social nature was changed, in other words, she became obsessed,
as did others in the days of Christ, and the manifestations of the
once gentle woman was changed to that of a demon—uncontrolable
by any moral persuasion and ready to spill her husband's heart's blood.
I could relate many such cases if space would permit, and only give
these to illustrate a principle.

Again, there are entranced mediums who, before public audiences,
will discourse most elegantly and beautifully upon the laws of love,
harmony, and kindness ; whom, while before the public, you would
almost think were angels from heaven ; but when followed from the
desk to the domestic relation, show by their lives the awful reality
of the opposite extreme. Damnation in all its horrors is freely dealt
out around the family altar ; the vilest epithets and severest insults
are heaped upon their companions, and in the hour of physical anguish not one consoling word is given—even a cup of water would
be withheld to increase the sufferings. This condition of things continues year after year.

The question naturally arises in every mind if evil spirits can
communicate. Cannot good one's also ? I answer, that it will be
found to be a law of spiritual life, that the lower the spirit in the
scale of development, or the more intense their evil, the greater their
power to convert to their use the vital and magnetic forces of the
circle, or those more material elements which belongs to the earth
life ; and by making use of these forces they are enabled to subju-
gate the will of such as become mediums and hold them in mental
and physical vassilage. It is from this cause that all our physical
manifestations are from such low order of spirits, many of which
are so material that they are able almost to project themselves visi-
bly and tangibly into the external world.

Entrancement is unnatural and, therefore, disorderly. God never designed, as an orderly condition, that one mind should be held in subjugation to another, whether in or out of the body. Therefore, I do not believe that any pure and elevated spirit ever entranced a mortal medium. They may be, and often times are, sophistically intellectual ; but generally quite as well pleased with contention, vulgarity, and profanity as with anything of a more serious nature. Truly elevated spirits do not entrance, write, paint, draw, or in any way move physical substances ; but they may, and undoubtedly do, cast a gentle and almost unperceived impression upon the mind, which so mingles or blends with our own that it becomes a part of ourselves. We feel its inspiration, and like the approach of the imperceptible morning dawn and the gradual coming on of the twilight hour, we cannot point out the precise time it commenced, or when it withdrew its genial influence. This is the highest and truest order of mediumship ; then the next is an influx manifesting itself in admonishing or prophetic dreams ; next visions, then trances, and so down to the lowest order, the moving of physical substances. I think we here have a true scale of the character of spirits which manifest themselves. I do not wish to be understood that persons upon any plain may not become clairvoyant and able to see spirits corresponding to their own condition. But when John W. Edmonds leans back in his rocking chair, closes his eyes and says : " I s-e-e b-e-a-u-t-i-f-u-l a-n-d e-l-e-v-a-t-e-d s-p-i-r-i-t-s," and then adds : " I wish they would stop that damn noise in the street, I can't see beautiful spirits when they are making such a devilish racket," it becomes simply ridiculous ; and we are forced to the conclusion that his apparent vision is the psychological result of his own egotism rather than any reality.

It would be folly to deny that there are multitudes of communications which are high in their moral tone, and apparently intended for our good. So with our healing mediums. I know that there are some actual cures made. But the question is, What is the object of this, admitting our theory of evil influences is correct ? We answer, to secure confidence. If all communications bore upon the face of them the impress of devils, we should have no hesitation in rejecting them, and thus they would lose their dominion over us. Therefore, they administer to us their moral poisons, mingled with the sweets of good and truth ; and when they have thus sufficiently impregnated our souls and weakened our moral constitution they take us as willing victims into captivity. Such, also, is exactly the case with the most of our healing mediums. Intensely wicked themselves their bodies are used by demons as external magnetic batteries to infuse into their nostrums and patients the most morally perverting and physically destructive influences. The public will yet awaken to a consciousness of an enormous evil in this direction. Their own bodies are infused with an infernal aurer which is freely imparted to everything with which they come in contact, and the susceptible and impressable patient is magnytized into a like condition. Many of them may justly be named as the mild-posts to perdition.

After saying this much in reference to the class of spirits which are allied to this sphere, we will proceed to speak briefly of the mediums they use to externalize their influences.

If we commence with the Fox family in 1848, and critically investigate all the various mediums of both sexes up to the present time, we shall find slight shades of difference according to their own inherent natures, but nearly all traveling in one grand march to ruin—their music is the wails of sufferings which their moral desecrations have created ; their captain, the Arch Fiend ; their legion of honor, prowling monsters ; their battle field the hearts of humanity, and the holy institutions of God. They hoist any banner which may for the time best suit their purpose, and their captives are made their fit companions, only when their moral vision is destroyed and their hearts are torn out. Nearly all of them, soon after yielding themselves up to spirit control, become wholly reckless of every moral, social and religious obligation. In other words, they become a fortress, built out into the external world, inhabited by demons. And their career is just such as we could reasonably expect, dictated by evil genii, who can bring to their aid the experience of centuries.

It is a startling reality, visible to all who will open their eyes to see, that nearly all mediums, especially those for mental manifestations, become wholly disqualified for the continuance of any practical relations of life ; and there is among them a perpetual tendency to form extra-marital relations. As companions, they are ardent and affectionate, but a single day may, and often does, suffice to change their whole moral nature, and transform their love into the most bitter of all hatreds. In other words, they are what the magnetism of their surroundings, or their controlling demons see fit to make them ; and, therefore, as unreliable as is the influence brought to bear upon them.

I will now proceed to prove the proposition stated in the commencement of this chapter, viz : that spiritual control degrades the morals, and destroys the perception of justice and honor. Facts are worth more than theories, and, therefore, we shall present a few of such cases as stand prominent before the world. We shall purposely avoid reference to those who are in the ardency, instability and indiscretion of youth ; but take veterans in experience, and whose characters were well established antecedent to their becoming Spiritualists. By so doing, no one can accuse us of unfairness.

John M. Spear, of Boston, over fifty years of age, many years a clergyman of high moral standing, was extensively known as the Prisoners' Friend, and the John Howard of America. I knew him well, antecedent to his becoming a Spiritualist, and he was almost universally acknowledged a paragon of almost every Christian virtue. He has now been nine years a medium. His family is broken up, and the wife, to whom he was once a most worthy husband, is forsaken ; he is traveling with his paramour who acts as his scribe in reporting his spiritual lectures, and, last Fall, bore to him what they call a spiritual baby—but of sufficient materiality to counterbalance nine pounds. To show the extent of his infatuation, I quote, from memory, from one of his lectures :—" Cursed be the marriage institution ; cursed be the relation of husband and wife ; cursed be all who would sustain legal marriage. What if there are a few tears shed, or a few hearts broken, they only go to build up a great principle, and all great truths have their martyrs."

Rev. S. C. Hewit, a man of brilliant intellect and high moral purposes and social standing, aged about fifty, commenced publishing a Spiritual paper in Boston, in 1852, since which time he has been a Spiritual Lecturer. In 1858, he left an invalid wife in a water cure, in Cleveland, Ohio, and started out on a lecturing tour, with a Miss ——, and soon after addressed a letter to his wife, stating that he had found his true " spiritual affinity," and that she must cease to longer look upon him as her husband. His " affinity" in turn soon left him, so I am credibly informed.

Hon. John W. Edmonds, of New York, is sufficiently advanced in years to have his inherent character well established. He has occupied high and responsible positions, which he has most honorably filled. Thus far he was justly entitled to public confidence and respect. As near as I am able to learn, he has been a medium since 1852 ; and how far he has lost all reliability and moral consciousness, I leave for the reader to decide upon the evidence which will be presented in the next chapter.

Dr. Geo. T. Dexter, the well known associate of Edmonds, in the publishing of his works on Spiritualism, and through whom much of the matter was given, and whom I once well knew as a highly respectable physician, in Lancaster, N. H. ; separated from his wife and family ; suddenly left the city for parts unknown, in consequence of having been accused of a crime which I forbear to mention.

Rev. J. S. Loveland, formerly a Methodist clergyman in Charlestown, Mass., now a Spiritual lecturer, abandoned his wife, and resides at the cess-pool of Free-Loveism, called *Modern Times*, on Long Island.

P. B. Randolph, a popular Spiritual Lecturer, abandoned his wife and children, married another woman who, in turn soon abandoned him, and he attempted suicide ; finally embraced religion, usurped the control of his own mind, confessed his faults and delusions, and like a true and honorable man, returned to the bosom of his family. In this last act he has set a worthy example for others.

Dr. Brookie, a prominent medium, was caught in bed with the wife of his friend, and was most terribly whipped. So says the Cincinnati papers.

Isaac Harrington, formerly a Baptist clergyman in good standing, and one of the strongest mediums I ever met with, was abandoned by his wife, who was also a medium ; he took another woman and left the country and his children.

Hon. Warren Chase, one of the most noted Spiritual Lecturers, separated from his wife, and whose character is too well known to need comment. In his published letters in the Spiritual papers, he earnestly recommends the "free love" association on Long Island as an interesting home for Spiritualists. Like the sailor, he finds a temporary wife in every Spiritual port, "from Maine to the Mississippi."

Mrs. E. J. French of this city, a trance speaker and medical medium, left a most worthy husband in Pittsburg, Pa., of whom she was not worthy, and now lives with a Mr. Thomas Culbertson, who also left his wife ; and of whom Prof. James J. Mapes has rooms and partial board.

Mrs. A. L. Gilman, a medium of this city, left her husband, and he procured a divorce on the proof of adultery ; and he informs me that she is now living with her paramour, who is a married man and a Spiritualist.

Mrs. Amanda M. Britt, a very popular speaking medium, and once a highly worthy and intelligent woman, personally informed me that her conjugal relations were the most happy of earth. She suddenly became estranged from her worthy husband, left him and soon after married another man.

Mrs. Ada L. Coan, of New York, the most popular test medium in the United States, lived in the utmost harmony with her husband for a few years, and a more worthy man does not exist, but suddenly, without any apparent cause, she abandoned him. As the abandonment is recent, I can only add that but a short time antecedent to the separation, she manifested the strongest affection for him. But the most unnatural feature was that she left him while he was laboring under a severe chronic indisposition at a time when his life was nearly despaired of. Inhuman indeed !

J. H. W. Toohey, a Spiritual Lecturer, and once editor of a Spiritual paper, left his wife and went West and procured a divorce.

Mrs. Albertson, a very beautiful and highly accomplished lady, and one of the most powerful mental mediums in this country, left her husband, a highly respectable lawyer once of this city, and now changes her "affinities" with almost every new moon, sometimes more frequent.

Mrs. Julia Branch, a very susceptible medium, left two husbands, and is now living with the free-lovers in this city. But it is useless to proceed, the catalogue is endless.

John Hewes, Dr. Curtiss, and Mr. Fairbanks of this city, and Hattie Eager of Boston, committed suicide in consequence of Spiritual infestation.

I commenced writing this work with the full determination to publish the names of all the mediums, as far as I could ascertain, who had broken off their marital relations. But on investigating the matter still further, I find this *startling fact*, (viz.,) we have more than four hundred public mediums and Spiritual lecturers in the northern States. At least three hundred of them have been married. Nearly one-half of these have absolved their conjugal relations ; a large proportion of the remainder are living in the most discordant relations, having abandoned the bed of their partner ; many cohabiting with their "affinities" by the mutual consent of husband or wife ; and a still greater number living in promiscuous concubinage. This general statement includes all phases of mediumship, such as, rapping, tipping, writing, healing, speaking, clairvoyant, trance, etc., etc.

From these facts the reader will see how utterly impossible it would be for any one to make out anything like a definite list of the several conditions. But those already given will be sufficient to show the general medley of moral corruption. The different phases of mediumship proves disastrous just in proportion as it rises to the *mental powers.* The tipping and rapping are at one extreme, and the unconscious entrancement at the other. Among the latter, moral ruin proves to be quite universal, and I think it will be found on a critical investigation, that no trance medium has ever gone before the public and maintained an upright and honorable life. I called upon Mrs. W. R. Hayden, a lady cf high merit, who has set a worthy example of fidelity to her nuptial vows, and who is extensively known both in this country and Europe as a physical medium—she frankly confessed to me that she knew of no trance medium who had perpetuated their conjugal relation. This certainly speaks volumes of the moral and social bearings of Spiritualism. I knew of two or three in private life where the marriage is not yet absolved, but the entrancements are of recent date, and therefore offer no exception to this rule. It will be understood that I am speaking only of those who occupy a public position, and there we shall find conjugal infidelity as universal as entrancement. In private life, also, the same difficulty is increasing with an alarming rapidity, so much that conjugal harmony is becoming the exception and not the rule among Spiritualists. The more I investigate this matter the more terrible it appears. The infatuation becomes so strong that even their ruin does not awaken them to a realization of the nature of the influence brought to bear upon them. Like the charmed bird they seek their own destroyer, and fondly flutter into the gaping pit, which is ready to pierce them with its deadly fangs, and poison the blood which courses every avenue of their being. Go to the men and women who have thrown off all the restraints which regulate a healthy society, and ask them if they have been benefitted by Spiritualism, and the following will be the substance of their reply :—" Yes, Spiritualism has freed me from the bigotry and superstitions of Christianity ; it has convinced me that the Bible is a record of events of no more importance than those which are daily occurring around us—that it is the work of designing priests, and wholly unreliable, and as such should be discarded ; it has convinced me of the importance of a cultivation of all my faculties, sexual as well as the moral and religious—that marriage can never continue beyond the duration of the affections, and if another can develop in me more love than my husband or wife, in virtue of that very love I am newly married, and the old should be absolved, for we should be true to nature, and no law has any right to interfere in my affections." These deluded victims call this state of religious and social depravity, " progression."

I insert the following letter without a change of a word, written to a medium, a gentleman's wife, by Augustus T—r, a man of some fifty years of age, and, at the same time, blessed with a most excellent wife and a family of children. The Spirits had declared these parties to be spiritually *man* and *wife*. Her husband finally procured a divorce on the proof of adultery. The letter will need no comment.

TUESDAY MORNING, 13 January, 1857.

DEAREST DEAR ONE.

PET WIFE.—I cannot send the first sheet off without pouring out my further feelings, and say, I went to a circle last evening hoping I might get something from you; but doomed to a disappointment. So many and most skeptics, and you know my friends cannot come under such difficulties, so I returned home at 10 o'clock again. The girls and Dewitt went to Buckley's, and they had got home before me. All retired to get up early, as they were to leave by the early train to Waterford; so I am again alone, and I am not sorry, as my mind is too full of thoughts of you to be happy, with any to intrude upon them. To-morrow eve Miss Hardinge gives a musical and tableau entertainment, and all the Spiritualists are to attend, so I hear, and Mr. Eighle and myself will attend; and so I try to pass off the time. How it drags its weary length along, and, *dear one*, your sufferings must be more than mine I even fancy, as you cannot escape, but are caged; and as you write he has returned, broke down at the mill, and his health broke down also. Poor man! he is to be pitied; and if he is to be removed, and you freed, that will somewhat repay you for your sacrifice; then you cannot blame yourself, and others cannot say ought about your leaving him. You say again you are impressed he will not live long; you know, dearest, your impressions are generally nearly all right—and may they prove so in this case, as I think all will be more happy, and I know you and myself will be, and much of your trouble will be removed. Shall we yet be joined together here on this earth, and no one to molest us? Have Spirits told you so? Certainly, they have told me we were joined together, and let no man put us asunder. Other mediums have said there was, while you are absent, a chain of light emanating from me to you, and it never *would* or *could* be broken, and through Mag, and from her own mother, I was told I must not murmur as a part of myself was gone from me, as it would be returned again, and I would be made whole, and said much that consoled me at the time; and then I thought you would soon be returned to me again. But soon, *dear angel pet*, may be soon to them, but eight months is, to me, *long*, and from your situation I conceive you think so too; but, dearest, let us pray and wait the time out allotted us. Spring—*sweet April*. May the wings of time speed faster, yea, faster than ever before, and that gladsome sound of the songster arrive, not only to gladden nature, but our weary, worn, lowly spirits, and all may work together for good and our happiness, and the happiness and elevation of others, both here and in the spirit world—a mission I love to assist in doing—and may holy angels guide and guard us, and give you strength to bear up under all your trials, and be returned back again to the heart who will greet it, and clasp it in fond, speechless embrace, and implant upon its sweet lips as pure and loving kisses as ever mortal could, or ever did implant. I will write you each week, dear one, and send two papers, *Write often*, dearest wife; and I remain *thine—yes, thine forever*, your ever firm friend and lover.   GUS.

The sacredness of Divine Revelation, which is the soul of all good, and marriage, which is the embodiment, are discarded ; the first as a libel on common sense, and the latter as an outrage on freedom. Thus deprived of both soul and body, they become as moral excrescences which have grown up out of decaying materials, where the laws of heaven have ceased to operate to produce order and harmony. Instead of soaring aloft into the region of the moral and religious sentiments, and viewing the world from its Pizgar's heights, they sink to the muddy pools and meandering streams, filled with every hideous reptile, which flows through the valley of inverted passions. As the pall of gloom draped the world during the "Dark Ages," by the rejection of the Bible, so this people are overshadowed by all the evils, miasmas, and fogs which have arisen from an infernal intercourse—the intellect bewildered, the moral sentiments perverted, while the passions are lashed into the wildest fury.

The best and most critical minds in the Spiritualist ranks, are beginning to fully realize that this converse with spirits, would, if left to its free course and work out its designs, result in the destruction of all bonds of society ; stir up the vilest animosities ; destroy all human confidence ; ignore all religion, and totally destroy the institutions of marriage, and open every flood-gate of iniquity. All who have yielded themselves to its influence and teaching have run the same sad course, slightly varied according to circumstances, but the end thereof has been death. The end is not yet. The most terrible consequences will yet grow out of this infatuation of listening to and absorbing the sophistry of demons, believing it to come from angels. Some are sanguine in their conviction that they are holding communion with the wise and good, some with the apostles, others with Jesus Christ, and still others with God himself. Thus, these teachings become to them the highest authority, and they are such as lay the ax at the root of every healthy regulation of society. Adultery, to effect a greater degree of spiritual and physical development—the breaking up of marriage to aid in a more perfect unfoldment—become to them mandates from heaven, which must be obeyed. Human authority becomes feeble and futile when compared with the Divine ; and reason yields its throne to this infatuation.

In 1853 Mr. John F. Whitney, now editor of the *Pathfinder*, established rooms at No. 553 Broadway, New York, for the benefit of public investigation of Spiritualism ; and at the same time commenced the publishing of a weekly Spiritual paper. This was the origin of the association known as the " Society for the Diffusion of Spiritual Knowledge," which was carried on at the expense of some *two hundred dollars* per week. The members of this society have nearly all gone the road to destruction. One fled the country to escape imprisonment ; another inquires of the spirits for the condition of his illegitimate children ; the third books his name with another man's wife, and she a medium, at one of our hotels as man and wife, and both occupy the same room ; another commits the vilest fraud ; another was indicted for perjury and also commits adultery ; another openly advocates the most damning licentiousness, and still another engaged in the sacrilegious mission of breaking up families and thereby ruining young wives ; and whose head has already become covered with the mould of ripened iniquity, whose heart festers corruption from its own rottenness, and whose form has become the doleful sepulchre of its already morally dead spirit. The strongest mediums in the country were employed by this society to give test to the public. Mr. Whitney was, therefore, placed in the very heart of Spiritual intercourse, and had the most favorable opportunity of judging of its nature and influence. I quote from an article from his pen bearing date December, 1856, which has just been put into my hands. The reader cannot fail to see how closely his observation and experience corresponds with my own, and which most fully sustains every position I have taken. Multitudes who have been staunch friends and close observers of Spiritualism, have retired in disgust after witnessing its abominations, but to subsequently prevent the knowledge of their ever having been identified with it, they have not left their experience upon record. Mr. W. says :—

"We have seen much, and have passed through experience dearly bought, and that experience has taught us that Modern Spiritualism is but the work of that class of spirits whom Christ compelled to quit the body of mortals and enter into the herd of swine. We have seen mediums who like Hattie Eager (this girl was a prominent medium and committed suicide in Boston,) were looked upon as the very type of perfection, who, when moving among Spiritualists would pass as the model of virtue and goodness, yet these very mediums were adulteresses and the secret aiders and abettors in the development of others in the same category of crime. We have seen this not only in one instance but many. We have seen the husband and children deprived of wife and mother by the commands and direction of a spirit, purporting to be the deceased mother, under the plea that her child's progression on earth was retarded by moving in the sphere of her husband, and we have seen this progressive wife and medium become the mistress of another, and he a married man, and her course approved by the spirits, not only through one medium but a dozen— the same *guardian spirit* communicating the same approval through them all. We have seen the reformed Magdalene prostitute herself after her delivery from the haunts of sin, to the sensual appetites of a man calling himself a medium, and this man a husband and father, and she a highly developed medium, doing this under the direction of her spirit mother, and spirits known on earth as philanthropists and christians. We have seen the medium who, according to Spiritualists, was the paragon of virtue and perfection, and through whom spirits would discourse most beautifully and often bring tears to the eyes of those who composed the circle—we have seen this model of supposed virtue making love to a husband and father, and poisoning his mind to the merits and worth of his own wife. We have seen this model of supposed perfection also corresponding and engaging herself for a matrimonial union at the same time to another. We have seen this medium who, not content with the misery she had created in one family, throwing herself into the arms of another married man, and by the power of sympathy and "affinity," as it is called by these devils, through mediums and represented to him she was his affinity, and he, a medium, reciprocated these advances. We, in short, have known this angelic medium, whom, to look upon, one would suppose the paragon of goodness, guilty of all we have stated, and at the same time secretly aiding and abetting others in violating their marriage vows, and fulfiling the spirit law of "affinity" and attraction. We have seen a medium who was employed, during the day, in giving communications to persons from the other world, on retiring with her widowed mother, use language and expressions which would well befit the Five Points. We have seen spirits giving communications through this medium to a gentleman stating that it was his departed wife, desiring that he should marry this medium. We have seen the medium whose voice was made eloquent by the spirits, who had left his wife, boast of his power over the gentler sex, and tell us how the female mediums were often sent to him by their spirit guides, that he might develop them in the manner that Potiphar's wife desired to be developed by Joseph. We have seen the grayhaired Spiritualist ask the spirits what would become of his illegitimate children in the other world, and have heard him told one good deed would counter-balance an evil one; that by giving the medium money who was in want, he would thereby offset a bad deed by a good one.

We have seen and discerned rascality enough, growing out of Spiritualism, to convince us there is no good in it, *but that its whole tendency is to debase and demoralize those who embrace it.* We again warn the community to avoid and flee from it as they would from the most loathsome and disgusting disease, and these pests of society, the devil's agents, styled mediums (although some may be influenced by a sincere desire to obtain truth.) Death and hell are leagued with them; their power is mighty; they are soul and body bound to the car of Satan, and destruction, and misery are the followers of its course. Through fanaticism, deceit and hypocrisy, those dissemblers of virtue assume a sanctity and morality quite foreign to their nature, under the deceptive plea of development and progression—the hypocritical garb of purity and truth. Spirits through mediums gain the sympathy of mortals, and by false issues, false ideas and communications fasten the iron heel of death upon their victims, and suicide, insanity, and general *moral depravity* is the FINALE of their work."

Mr. Whitney can be assured that since he wrote this article, in 1856, the evils of which he speaks have increased, and become intensified beyond measure. The little rivulet springing from the mountain side, receives new accessions until it becomes a mighty torrent, triumphantly sweeping before it every opposing obstacle. So this evil is reaching a colossal power which, ere long, will be found to bear upon its polluted bosom the wrecks of millions. What a sad, social spectacle is here presented ; and that too, brought to pass in such a brief period of time ! Can the pages of history furnish a parallel ? The Bacchanalians of Rome, which disgraced humanity one hundred and eighty-six years before Christ, when the worst excesses, and most unnatural vices were indulged in by both sexes, may possibly have been a lower order of immorality than that which exists at present among Spiritualists. But the former numbered only about 7000, which were very few in comparison to the latter, and, therefore, of much less real public injury.

It will be borne in mind, that I have spoken mostly of public mediums, which are comparatively very few in number, and embraces only a small fraction of the whole difficulty. There are thousands of private mediums, and tens of thousands who eagerly drink in the same morally ruinous doctrines. When they can fully ignore all the wholesome regulations of society, and abandon themselves to evil, and licentiousness, they boastingly speak of their freedom from, what they call, social conventionalisms and the superstitions of Christianity. They plant themselves upon the *instincts* of their nature, and use their reason only to devise means for their gratification. In this way they invert the order of nature, and passion receives the approbation of conscience through a perverted intellect. In this state of mind, the wrongs which the world so deeply deplore, become, to them, a religion ; and as such all-powerful over them.

They earnestly contend that no external authority, and no code of human laws, can justly bind their affections, or interfere with their liberty to follow the impulse of their personal *affinities.* They claim that they have a God-given right to rectify any mistake they may have made, and do so as often as such mistakes occur ; and, therefore, in their affections, which they claim is the most important faculty of the human mind, they should be left to their own will, and seek such conjugal relation as, at the time, may best please them. There are multitudes who do not openly advocate, but who fully sanction this doctrine. In short this is the paramount doctrine of Spiritualism. They claim to be *monogamist*, because they have but one wife or husband at a time, though they may have a new one every day. Promiscuous concubinage, or free-loveism, belongs more exclusively to those who are most developed in Spiritualism. Socially, it is the inner sanctuary of the new philosophy to which all will arrive, when they become sufficiently harmonious or natural in all things. This much I most firmly believe, from a critical and extensive observation, that the Spiritualists, as a social body, are rapidly tending to a promiscuous relation of the sexes. The ultra free-lovers who have formed themselves into associations are aware of this fact, and they look upon the general introduction of Spiritualism as a John in the wilderness of conservatism, preparing the way for the reign of the kingdom of Lust. They see the general commotion in the spiritual ranks, and believe it to be the breaking-up of the fountains of the great deep of the marital relation ; and it is true, that it is showering upon them new victims, as frogs upon darkened Egypt. And when we see John W. Edmonds visiting and holding private circles with Kate Hastings, the most notorious wanton in New York, it clearly shows how little is virtue respected, and how great a leveler, not upwards but downwards, is Spiritualism.

I do not wish to be understood that there are no pure and good men and women who believe in spiritual intercourse. There are many whose inherent integrity even Spiritualism has not been able to destroy. Many of these already see the evil and give me a hearty " God speed" in my warning others to escape. Again, there are small classes of Christian Spiritualists springing up all over the country who believe in the Divine Revelations and the Unity of the Godhead—" that He exists in a Divine Trinity of Love, Wisdom and Operation, but that these are one, as the soul, spirit and ultimate spiritual body of man are one,"—that marriage is never to be annulled when consummated in freedom, except for the cause of natural adultery ; that regeneration is the end sought by all of God's dealings with mankind ; that by yielding ourselves up to evil and the dictation of spirits we become demons ; that these evil spirits assume deceptive appearances and resemble, at times, the most distinguished and illustrious members of the human race. They also personate good angels, take the likeness of our departed friends. The most abandoned of them attempt to personate the Lord—that disorderly Spiritualism is to be avoided and not sought, and that we should immutably plant ourselves upon the Holy Word, adhering to its doctrines and living a life of holy uses, and thus preparing ourselves to become angels, and to forever dwell with God.

I have said enough to show the Social, Moral and Religious bearings of Spiritualism—it reforms none, ruins many, financially, socially, morally, and religiously. The auroral beauty of the upheavings from the nether regions by the volcanic eruptions may dazzle and bewilder for awhile, but its melted lava spreads over the thickly peopled plains, and the rising morning sun looks upon ruin and desolation where once teemed life and animation. So with this vampire of Spiritualism, its infernal auror and delusive sophistry injected into the soul, like the serpant, charms for a season, and while we are intensely gazing at this new wonder, we are overwhelmed and lost amidst its ruins ; and when the Sun of Righteousness sheds His genial light upon us, we then behold the awful desolation it has caused. Reason perverted, conscience misled, virtue abandoned, character ruined, families broken up, hopes blasted, and universal chaos and confusion everywhere surround us. Can we ask for more evidence to prove from whence this evil comes ? What ripened fruits does it bring forth but damnation ? The apparent good is only the golden goblet which contains the deadly poison, and he who drinks thereof will surely die. Oh, God ! heart-felt thanks, spontaneously well up from the depths of my soul for timely deliverance, and that I was protected though ruin everywhere surrounded me. May my gratefulness be manifest by love to Thee, and a life of holy uses ; and in Thine own time cause Thy Divine Spirit to permeate the heart of her whom Thou once gave to bear with me the joys and sorrows of life. Drive back every infesting influence and free her otherwise pure and gentle spirit from all that would seek her harm, and may she yet become a channel for Thy Divine influence to sustain and uphold Thy holy institutions.

CHAPTER II.

THE HATCH DIVORCE CASE.

In many of its features this is, unquestionably, one of the most remarkable cases ever brought before a legal tribunal. It presents a great degree of depravity, and a loss of moral consciousness seldom equalled in the history of legal jurisprudence, and forensic knowledge sitting in judgment, prostituted to the vilest and most unnatural purposes. In other words, it is *Spiritualism*, not merely blossomed out, but gone to seed. If it be true that evil genii have anything to do with the events of this life, there can be only one possibility of their having any regret in this affair, (viz.,) that they have been outdone in iniquity. The reality of the case can never be fully drawn by the pen. It will be painted by the interior consciousness upon the inner wall of the temple not made with hands, and there alone can its deformity duly impress the soul. The world has not been prepared for such extremes, and therefore can have but feeble conception of this case. I cannot but expect that a fair and truthful statement will be regarded as an exaggeration unwarrantable. Aware of this I shall draw the colors as dimly as I can, and not withhold the facts.

I had seen something of the dangers and unreliability of mediumship, antecedent to Miss Cora L. V. Scott becoming my wife ; but I had but faint conception of its extent. Separations and divorces were fully discussed between us, and the consummation of our nuptials was made conditional, that no subsequent events should ever absolve the union. We mutually and solemnly pledged ourselves before God and to each other, that our union should be life-long, regardless of all moral and social conditions,—that if either lacked in moral force, the other should, with redoubled energy, seek to make up the deficiency, and reform the offender. Also that we would mutually study the happiness, each of the other, to the fullest extent of our abilities ; errors should be reformed, offences, if any, atoned for, pardon freely bestowed ; believing that by so doing we could reap the richest harvest of conjugal enjoyment. Freely pledged to these conditions our nuptials were consummated. For two years the auroral beauty of the morning sun of peace and happiness shone upon us. No clouds of darkness overshadowed us, no mumbling thunderings of discord greeted our ears. We felt and believed ourselves more than blessed, and each day seemed to add new joys to our already happy existence. Alas, it was too great to continue! It was like the quiet repose which precedes the earthquake that smacks its mumbling lips o'er a doomed city. The transition was sudden and complete ; and a single hour forever buried our every joy. The black pall of slander trails o'er the corpse of ruined hopes, and the solidified monument of disgrace will ere long mark the tomb of blighted vows.

On the morning of the 23d of July, 1858, I left Mrs. Hatch in Brooklyn, and started for Chicago, Illinois. The 25th she wrote me the following letter :—

BROOKLYN, Sunday, July 25, 1858.

My Dear Frank :—Doubtless you will expect a letter from me before this reaches you, but when I say that physical indisposition has prevented me from writing sooner, I think you will consider it sufficient apology. I am still with Mrs. Taylor, who has treated me with the same motherly tenderness that always characterizes her. I missed you more than I can tell during those hours of pain and suffering, but kindly hands and hearts ministered to my every want. This week I shall be busily employed in sewing, but cannot tell when I shall meet you until I receive a letter from you, which shall indicate the probable length of time it will require for you to complete your business. Mr. and Mrs. Ludden called here last evening ; he cannot yet decide whether they will be able to go to Niagara or no. Mr. Sollace, his partner, is better than when he left, and hopes to become convalescent very soon. I suppose you will write me concerning my dear mother and her future prospects. She has suffered much and should be repaid by constant love and attention from her children. I suppose you are rusticating in the quiet retreat of Wynnetca. Please to remember me in all kindness to Dr. and Mrs. Abell. When you call at Mr. Richmond's, present to the family, individually and collectively, my kindest regards. I would like much to see them. 'Tis about one year since we were there, is it not?

I know of nothing that will interest you, not having seen any body or heard any news. I shall probably go to Mr. Ludden's to-morrow and there spend the week, or wait a letter from you to decide upon my future course. I seem to feel the melancholy impression that you will be longer detained than was anticipated. Slowly drag the hours away, but I will try and be patient. I shall expect from you a full account of your journey, and hope to get a letter Monday. Write in reply to this if possible. And now, *Dear Frank,* as I know you abhor lengthy effusions, I will not inflict you with any further remarks. Imagine, my dear, all I would say in conclusion, and believe me as ever, your devoted   CORA."

On the 4th of August she again wrote me that she would meet me in Buffalo unless she received from me a telegraphic dispatch to the contrary. I returned the following dispatch—"Remain where you are, and I will be with you to-morrow." I was informed that on receiving this communication she danced with joy that we were so soon to meet. On my arriving in Brooklyn, the 6th of Aug., she was at dinner, and saw me pass the window, and rushed from the basement to the parlor with all possible speed, and for a moment gave me as warm a greeting as ever a husband received from a wife. But an apparent indifference soon followed, and within ninety minutes from that time she informed me that she " Did not wish any longer to remain my wife." I required the reasons for such a declaration. I will here record the dialogue which followed, which, on her part, was carried on in the same prompt and decisive manner which characterizes her before audiences.

Dr. Why, Cora ! on what do you predicate such a decision ?

Cora. Well, I have three reasons.

Dr. I will hear them.

C. 1st, I cannot sustain sexual relations with you without injury to myself.

Dr. However much I may differ with you in opinion, your person shall be held inviolate to the end of any period of time you may designate.

C. That is all I can ask, and that objection becomes removed.

Dr. What is your second reason ?

C. You are closer in your money matters than I wish you were.

Dr. Have I not supplied all your wants ?

C. Yes, far more prodigally than I would myself.

Dr. Have I not paid my debts ?

C. I do not know that you owe a dollar in the world.

Dr. As I have supplied all your wants, and paid all my bills, what more do you ask ?

C. Well, it is the general impression that you are penurious.

Dr. You are aware that any such impression has not grown out of any lack of expenditure, but wholly from our having been successful, in our business, and the envy of unimportant parties. But what is your third reason ?

C.—You do not take the interest in my mother that I wish you to.

Dr.—Have I not supplied your mother's wants as far as I know them ?

C.—Well, you have assisted her, but she requires a *home*.

Dr.—And for this end I have diligently labored to procure means that we might all have a home together. Your mother has positively refused any liberal donations from me, and has freely expressed her desire that I should retrench my expenses, both upon you and in other ways, and save our means to purchase a residence.

C.—Well, there is no use in discussing tho matter—my mind is made up.

Dr.—Are these all the reasons you have for breaking up your conjugal relation ?

C.—*They are.*

Dr.—To me they are small in the extreme. I could not have ex·pected it from you, neither do I believe that the world will justify you in your course.

C.—I think that they are sufficient, and I believe that you will find that tho world will so regard them.

Here ended the conversation for that time. I saw her sad condition, and my soul was torn asunder with anguish.

At this time, Mrs. Hatch's most intimate friend, from Buffalo, was in this city, and had spent several days with her during my absence. I enquired of her if Cora had informed her of her determination to absolve her marriage. She informed me that she had not. But, on the contrary, "supposed she was the best satisfied of any woman in the world." The next day Cora accompanied me to New York, where we again met this lady, who then advised her not to leave her husband. I well remember Cora's reply, which was given in much apparent astonishment.—"*Leave my husband !* I have no such idea nor never had such a thought. *It shall never be said of me that I ever left my husband.*" At intervals she would appear to be her self again, and would come to me with all the ardency and warmth of her former affection ; but these grew less, and by the fourth day they had entirely ceased.

No person was ever more completely transformed. Every vestige of the former Cora, in all her affectional and social nature towards me, was gone ; and I verily believe that no pleasure would have been greater to her, than to have seen me carved in pieces before her eyes, or torn limb from limb by some infernal machine. That great *intensity* of her nature which has caused her to be so much admired in her social relations and intellectual efforts, was turned into wrath and vengeance towards me. At a time when she appeared to be the most normal, I inquired if she had any thing against me, or, if I had not always treated her with the utmost kindness, and done all I could for her happiness and prosperity. The following is the reply, which I wrote down at the time :—" No, sir. As a moral man, as a social man, and as an intellectual man, one whose ideas most fully correspond with my own, I have no objection to you, and should be as much pleased with your acquaintance and association, and should be as glad to treat you as a lady should treat a gentleman as any man in the world, but as a husband, I *hate* you."

This separation was so sudden and without any visible cause, that a multitude of various conjectures sprang up, and soon took the form of authentic reports, and thus the vilest calumny was freely circula-ted in every direction. The rotten hearted and demonized men and women eagerly sought for and absorbed these into their own being, as would a Jackall, decaying flesh. Cora knew their falsity, but smiled at their promulgation. I became almost frantic with suf-fering.

In this condition I first called upon James J. Mapes to aid me in staying my beloved wife in her mad career. I saw him immediately after having his first interview with her, and he exclaimed : " My God, Hatch, I am more excited than you are ! I never saw a woman so perfectly hallucinated in all my life. There is no reasoning with her. Every argument falls powerless at her feet."

About this time I wrote to Judge Edmonds, informing him of Cora's condition. The following is his reply :

LAKE GEORGE, August 20, 1858.

DOCTOR HATCH : I am very sorry, but not surprised to hear of Cora's indisposition. It is the result of my observations and experience, that mediums for mental manifestations cannot with safety be overworked.

The draft on the vital energies is very great, and unless properly regulated such mediumship is likely to be injurious.

Sometimes it affects the physical health as in the cases of Miss Hardinge and Miss Sweet; and sometimes the moral as in the case of Cora and some others.

Having regarded this as a truth, I have been very careful in that respect with Laura. I have watched closely her condition at times, and whenever I saw any signs of overworking, I have insisted on her stopping for a week or two at a time, and taking rest and recreation. I have then insisted upon an entire cessation during the warm weather. Hence it is I provided this rest of two months in the country, and thus it is I have preserved her powers and condition unimpaired.

Last Summer my admonition to cease in May was neglected, and importunity of friends yielded to instead. The evil consequences were soon manifest, and I know no exception to the rule.

The remedy in Cora's case is rest, time and recreation. She ought now for at least two months to spend her time in pleasant society, in agreeable scenery, and with an entire cessation of all spiritual influence. She will then recover a sound frame of mind.

I shall be in town on Monday next and will be glad to see you, and in conversa-tion enter more into detail than I can do in the limits of a letter. Yours, &c.,

J. W. EDMONDS.

The day I received the above letter I also saw the Judge, and he then informed me that he had conversed with his spirit friends and they assured him that Cora's condition was the result of an overtax-ed brain which weakened her physically, and evil influences had got possession of her, and that he could render me assistance in regain-ing control of her, and thus remove her from her present surroundings into a quiet retreat in the country. I assured him that while she appeared perfectly sane upon all other subjects there was no argument or persuasion which could reach her in her conjugal relation.

After due deliberation we devised the plan of an "arbitration," simply to induce her to pledge herself, and thus enable me to remove her without any arbitrary force. A bond of the most extreme character, to meet her disordered state of mind was drawn up by Mapes, which according to its letter gave them power to break up my family, confiscate my property, and blast my reputation, and at the same time screened them from any obligation to give any reasons whereof they had decided. J. W. Edmonds, James J. Mapes, and Dr. A. D. Wilson were selected as arbitrators. Whatever the decision might be, it placed her under no obligation which her marriage vows did not cover. This was that she might be induced to sign it.

After this sham arbitration had gone on for some two weeks, and I discovered the dishonest manner which they were conducting it, and their evident intention to increase rather than diminish the difficulty, I called upon each of them in person and informed them that I would stay proceedings unless they would pledge their honor that they would be governed by the laws of this State in their decision. Dr. Wilson gave me the required pledge. Mapes went still further, and said that he did not think it expedient for husband and wife to separate, even for adultery. I presume his wife is of the same opinion. Edmonds' statement will appear in the correspondence.

Mrs. H. and myself were not permitted to meet before them, and I was positively denied a copy of her complaint. For nearly two months they sought witnesses, with the pledge to them that I should not be present nor subsequently question them upon what they might testify to. The testimony of one was that I had, eighteen months previous, refused to furnish a party with an oyster supper; another that he had paid more stage fares for me than I had for him; another, that Mrs. Hatch had called upon her one damp day without rubbers; another, that he had once heard me make a vulgar expression while walking with him. Nothing revelant to the case before them appeared; and I most solemnly affirm that according to my best recollection the above were the strongest proofs before them. These men took the advantage of Cora's insane condition, and she was induced to meet them in Mapes' private room, (No. 8 Fourth Avenue) evening after evening, and relate to them all the particulars and minutiæ of her nuptial chamber in their most *disgusting details.* The damning horrors of that affair I have neither disposition, patience, or forbearance to rehearse. And still, I have only such as they related to me, which, doubtless, is only a moity of the reality. Thus I reposed confidence in these men, and trusted in their hands the most sacred relation of life, and it blasted and withered beneath their unhallowed and dastardly touch. She was made a victim of their infernal magnetism, and thereby became still more intensified in her purposes of wrong until she was carried beyond anything I could have conceived possible.

At my request, Edmonds invited Cora to accompany him home at the close of one of their meetings ; (for I then believed him to have some honor,) she did so, and was entranced the same evening, at his house, and made a speech, since which time he has manifested the greatest *malignity* towards me. I suppose that Cora knows as little of the nature of that interview as myself. We will pass by this arbitration as one of the dark deeds of a depraved humanity. The revelations of eternity will fully withdraw the curtain which covers its iniquity. Mapes had the principal, if not the entire management of the matter. At last they arrived at the conclusion, which evidently they commenced with, viz : that we must be separated, and so awarded. The following quotation from this wonderful document will unravel the mystery :

" We adjudge and determine that there is now in the hands of the said Benjamin F. Hatch, property and assets of the value of three thousand dollars, all of which is the proper earnings of said Cora, and of *right*, and according to *law*, belong to her as her separate property, all of which, however, she freely relinquishes to the said B. F. Hatch, except the sum of about *seven hundred dollars* now in the safe keeping of JAMES J. MAPES, which she claims and demands as her own, and we do accordingly award, order and determine, that the said sum of about seven hundred dollars does absolutely belong to her as her separate property, and shall be paid to her to the exclusion of any control over the same by her said husband."

SIGNED.   J. W. EDMONDS,
A. D. WILSON,
JAS. J. MAPES.

I loaned Mapes this money in personal friendship, and on the basis of his having assured me that he was worth fifty thousand dollars, but which I have since learnt is wholly *false ;* and, likewise, that an execution against him is *utterly worthless.* This money matter was kept wholly a secret from me, until I read the above award, never having been alluded to in the arbitration. Mrs. Hatch had previously told me that she did not wish for any money, that she could make all she desired. Subsequently she was over-persuaded by others to send in a request for the $700. I had notified Mapes that I should require the full payment immediately, as I desired to take Cora to Europe, in order to remove her from present influences. Thus my family was broken up and the money awarded to her, knowing that she would never enforce its payment. I sued him, and he replied by putting in the plea of *usury*. The usury portion of these notes were given in the financial crisis of the Fall of 1857, he stating, at the time, that he could make two per cent. per month more than he was paying me. Confidence, friendship, trust, and honor are all freely offered up, upon the altar of hypocritical fraud. It has been well said, " that any one who will outrage all those principles which lay at the foundation of all business and social transactions, it would require an archimedial lever, with heaven for its fulcrum, to pry him up to the moral standard of pirates and high-waymen." The latter will respect each others rights.

All the funds I could control I had invested on mortgage for two years, and relied upon this $700 to pay my current expenses. I had divided with Cora to the last dollar, and I could not raise ten dollars from Mapes. Thus I was left wholly without any available means. I have no censure to cast upon Dr. Wilson, for I believe he was honestly duped by Mapes. I called upon Dr. W. for the reasons of his decision, which he declined to give, also upon Mapes, and after some persuasion he made the following statement, to wit :—" One of the two reasons that caused that decision against you was, the two letters you published in the Banner of Light." One announcing my belief in obsessions by evil spirits, and the other, wherein I advocated the sanctity of the marriage institution ; fidelity to each other, and that nothing should be allowed to mar its beauty and harmony—which is not a very pleasing doctrine to Spiritualists—So in this I was a heretic. I then wrote to Edmonds to see if I could get some light upon the subject from that source ; and advised him to reconsider his decision. He replied to me by letter, which I publish entire, excepting less than two lines of printed matter, but of such a filthy nature as to be unfit for type, and grew out of their lecherous conversation in the arbitration ; but which is wholly false in any spirit of truth.

"Dr. HATCH:—I am not unwilling to state to you my reasons for my decision in the matter of your wife and yourself, nor am I desirous to withhold them from the world.

"I could not consent to decide that a young and delicate, and refined female should be compelled to live as a wife with a man who could : *First.* (omitted clause.)

"*Second :* When his wife had earned some $3,000 or $7,000 in the course of two years, when her husband had not earned one cent, would refuse to trust her with any amount, and thus confiscate to his own use the earning and property which, in fact, belonged to her and not to him—with which he had *nothing to do*, and which he could not control without a gross breach of confidence on his part.

"This $6,000 or $7,000 was hers and not yours. She entrusted you with it, and you, instead of consulting her wishes, confiscated it to yourself, and appropriated it to your own use. This you had no right to do, and I could not feel myself warranted in trusting you any further with her earnings or her property.

"*Third :* Who would, from a spirit of penuriousness, deny to his wife the comforts and necessaries of life, when he was dependent on her and her labors, and not on his own, for his daily bread. But for her you would have starved, and yet you denied her any control over her own. I could not consent to her longer being subjected to such a course of treatment.

"I have, therefore, nothing to reconsider, but insist that our judgment was right, and no other could have been arrived at by any right-minded man.

"Yours, &c.,   J. W. EDMONDS."

NOTE. No "cruel treatment" is here alluded to; a singular fact if her present allegation of personal abuse is true. She did not even allude to anything of the kind before the arbitrators. A wonderful omission !

This letter was published in the *New York Tribune*, with the following reply :—

To the Editor of the N. Y. Tribune.

SIR : I have felt myself called upon and have been frequently advised to publish the above letter, that the public may have the basis on which this noted Spiritualist pretends to justify himself in being instrumental in separating husband and wife. The letter will need no comment; but a statement of a few facts will be necessary, which I will give in this connection.

In reading the above most imbecile letter, one cannot well suppress a feeling of mirth, mingled with contempt—mirth for the arrogance, and contempt for the malicious and vindictive spirit manifested, and the utter falsehood of its every paragraph, as the reader will see by the following statement with which Edmonds was made fully acquainted.

It is well known that I married Cora when she was in very indigent and comparatively obscure circumstances, and, by constant and energetic toil on my part, combined with her own inherent powers, we succeeded in procuring for her no little notoriety. I spared no pains or expense to bring her before the public to the best possible advantage, and, in so doing, we were enabled to lay by nearly $3,000 in the "two years." My desire was that, in case I should be taken away, the entire proceeds should be her's; and, therefore, when we had accumulated $1,000, I purchased a piece of real estate in *her name* for *four thousand and four hundred dollars,* paid the $1,000, and gave my individual notes for the balance ; and when I visited Chicago in July last, (at which time she left me,) it was to make the first payment on these notes. In reference to "not trusting her with any amount," at all times there was in her trunk from $20 to $200, as much at her disposal as mine, which, however, she seldom made any use of, as all her wants were most bountifully supplied. So much for the honorable gentleman's "second " reason.

My "spirit of penuriousness," which denied to the wife the comforts and necessaries of life," is as follows : During the two years which I most happily spent with Cora, I paid *fourteen hundred dollars* for her clothing and jewelry, and there was no want of her's, great or small, made known to me which was ungratified, save one. That was that I should purchase a house for her mother, which I was wholly unable to do, and meet the payment of the notes which I had already given for her. The 22d of July, 1858, which was the day before my departure for Chicago, and the last day I lived with Cora, she went with me to A. D. Stewart & Co.'s. I requested her to call for whatever she desired, and after completing her purchases I asked if there was nothing more. She replied, "No, Frank, I cannot think of any other thing. I believe every want is supplied." My rule was to *anticipate* her wants as far as possible, and thus supply them before requested to do so. All who know her are aware that she is a walking contradiction to Edmond's "third reason.'

At the time of separation, in my criticism of her to ascertain the cause of her desire to break the nuptial vows, I asked her if I had not supplied all her wants. Her reply was as follows:—" Yes, *far more prodigally* than I would myself." Mrs. Hatch's mother has on several occasions reproved me for my prodigality in that direction, and thought it was a waste of money, which could result in no good to her daughter.

If our nuptial relations had been placed upon the basis of a pecuniary reward, instead of a harmonious and love union, I think that I may reasonably say that I have paid her five times as much as she could have made for herself. I most solemnly affirm that the first complaint which Cora ever made to me, to my present recollection, was when she informed me that she did not any longer wish to remain my wife. But on the contrary, had uniformly, in the strongest terms, expressed her entire satisfaction; not only to me but to all her friends, and that she was married for time and eternity. And she had repeatedly pledged herself to inform me if any custom or event should give her pain, that it might be remedied; for I was determined that no effort, on my part, should be spared to make her life blissful. My love for her made her pleasure mine.

Whether or no I should have "starved" during those two years without the assistance of my wife, I am unable to say. But as I have but little confidence in the profundity of the Judge's knowledge, I most respectfully decline reposing any confidence in that statement.

That "I had nothing to do with the *earnings* which all belonged to her," I can only say that I labored more days than she did hours in the accumulation. It was our *mutual business ;* and for the Judge to say that I had no moral or legal right to the "control of the proceeds without a gross breach of confidence on my part," shows him to be about as correct in legal matters as he is in his discernment of common justice.

That the Judge's letter to me is malicious and vindictive in its tone, imbecile in its character, and unmanly to the last degree in all its parts, needs no other proof than its perusal. "MOST NOBLE JUDGE, A DANIEL, A DANIEL, A SECOND DANIEL," *most truly.* Irony side. When persons, who have once occupied high and honorable positions, can so far bemean themselves as to become instrumental in breaking up family relations on such a basis, and that wholly false, as is set forth in Edmond's letter, it becomes us not to boast of the moral and elevating character of spiritual mediumship.

The other two arbitrators evidently felt disposed to take the more discreet part of withholding the grounds of their decision, and screen themselves behind what they believed to be a public prejudice against me for having made a little money out of spiritual lecturing, supposing that their position would secure for them and Mrs. H., the conviction of the public that I was guilty of some gross wrong against my wife. These men would enter the precincts of my family relation, and, while the hitherto devoted wife was laboring under an inversion of her conjugal feelings, produced by a too frequent entrancement (and which is as universal as spiritual control), and an overtaxed brain, or while a victim to unfortunate influences; and ruthlessly sever its once happy ties, try to confiscate my property, and, by implication, blast my character, and that, too, without feeling themselves called upon to give even the reasons whereof I was thus insulted and wronged.

I write thus plain and pointedly that I may, if possible, induce these men to manfully state any moral wrong which they are knowing to my ever having committed against my beloved but truant wife, Mrs. CORA L. V. HATCH. If they cannot do this, then they are morally bound to hide themselves in shame for the course they have pursued. I will wait a reasonable length of time for a reply.

Very truly,   B. F. HATCH, M.D.

New York, January, 1859.

To the Editor of the N. Y. Tribune.

SIR: I cannot consent to have any controversy with Dr. Hatch. He selected me as one of the arbitrators between him and his wife, and it is in no respect through my instrumentality or with my consent that the matter has been brought before the public. He, with your assistance, has done that; and you would not hear from me in the matter, if it were not for the fact that the letter from me to him, which you publish, has been so garbled.

I send you a true copy of my letter, that you may see how important a portion he has omitted, and what alterations he has made in it, to suit his own purposes.

I also send you a copy of his letter to which mine was a reply, and a statement of the charges, which we found were established against him. Thus you have the whole matter before you to do with it as you choose.

For my part I have done with it. No remarks of yours or his can, I think, provoke me to waste another word on the matter.

In the meantime you must allow me to add that I agree with you in the wish that this matter had been kept out of the papers, and that this is one of the many instances in which I have observed that the attempt to use Spiritualism for selfish purposes, is sure, first or last, to be attended with disastrous consequences.

New York, Jan. 4, 1859.   J. W. EDMONDS.

To the Editor of The N. Y. Tribune.

Sir: Some kind friend has forwarded me a copy of your paper of Jan. 5, containing a note from my friend J. W. Edmonds, in which he informs your readers that "he cannot consent to have any controversy with Dr. Hatch," and accuses me of having "garbled" his letter. I published *every word* of said letter except a brief paragraph, which would have made about two lines of printed matter, and which was of such a filthy character as to forbid its publication. Both Edmonds and a large class of the Spiritualist public will know that every paragraph of the published portion of that letter is an *entire falsehood*, which can be most fully substantiated beyond all controversy; and, notwithstanding this, he has the presumption to call upon the public to believe that there is truth in another statement of his, which is of such a nature it cannot be published. It only shows how readily a man may be induced to invent one wrong to screen himself from the just condemnation by the exposure of another. If he has any other "charges which were established against me," why not have given them to me as well as to the Tribune? Have I no moral right to know why my family is broken up and property confiscated? This very method of procedure is conclusive evidence of something deeply, morally wrong, and from which he cannot extricate himself with any degree of honor, and thus screens himself in the shades of silence. There were *no* charges sustained unless it be on the basis of her word in opposition to mine. Edmonds had frankly informed me that he had frequently been so infested by evil spirits that for days it wholly disqualified him for his avocation; and, out of charity to him, I had induced myself to believe that his letter to me was written while afflicted by one of those infestations, and that when he again became master of himself he would acknowledge his erring. Whether I was mistaken in my diagnosis or the obsession still continues, I know not.

Suffice it to say, that I have shown the *original* said letter to more than a dozen gentlemen, not one of whom would deem it any honor to be compared to Judge E. in judgment, accompanied by the same statement which I made to Edmonds, and upon which he claims to predicate the omitted brief paragraph, and they have uniformly expressed their condemnation in the strongest terms, and believed him to be either utterly incompetent of proper judgment upon the subject, or driven to the last extremity for self-justification in an unmanly cause. I will rest the entire case on the decision of three or five high-minded and honorable men, who are *unbribed*, whether I have committed any wrong in that matter, morally or socially. The fact is, it was only a most *miserable* and *dishonorable* subterfuge, which none but such would ever have resorted to.

That I have committed one great mistake since, not before the separation, I am free to acknowledge, and I am willing to receive its penalty. Christ was accused of casting out devils through Beelzebub the prince of devils. But he told them that "a kingdom divided against itself could not stand." Had he have called upon lascivious, profane and brandy-pickled men to perform the work of his holy mission, his folly would have been equalled only by that of B. F. Hatch.

The only basis of a separation between Mrs. H. and myself is *simply a desire on her part*, and that, too, which came upon her in a single day, unless her own written and verbal testimony previous to her inversion is to be totally disbelieved. The Free-Love doctrine is so prevalent among the Spiritualists that I suspected Mr. Edmouds with others of being tinctured with it. I therefore called upon him in person and gave him my apprehensions, and required a verbal pledge that he would be governed by the laws of the State in any decision he might make in my case, and distinctly stated that I would not permit him to act as an arbitrator on any other conditions. He evidently flew into a passion and said, "My opinions upon marriage are too well known to require any pledge from me, for I have stated in my public lectures on Spiritualism that I did not believe in a separation of husband and wife on any grounds whatever." And after making this statement with all the earnestness of a combative feeling, he then decides for a separation without "any grounds whatever," save the *desire* on her part. If he could not comply with the conditions, why did he ask to be put on that arbitration? He told me before I consented for him to act, that he had conversed with his spirit-friends, and that they had assured him that Cora's condition was solely the result of an over-taxed brain. He had also written me, from which I make the following extract: "I am sorry, but not surprised, to learn of Cora's indisposition. It is the result of my experience and observation that mediums for mental manifestations cannot with safety be overworked. * * The remedy, in Cora's case, is time, rest and recreation." I ask, in the name of all that is truthful, what confidence can I repose in a man thus vacillating?—who will tell me one thing one day, and another the next, and then resort to the most unjustifiable means to sustain his position? If I write plain, it is because that I have no patience with such vacillation and destitution of all the more noble qualities of true manhood, whether it be the result of Bacon, Swedenbourg or the Devil? *

Jan. 10, 1859.   Very truly,   B. F. HATCH, M. D.

This correspondence compelled them, in order to screen themselves from public condemnation, to resort to new measures. I had openly called upon them for the *cause* of their breaking up my family. They *had none to give;* and, therefore, Cora in her insane condition was induced to swear to a medley of unimportant and disgusting charges, as a complaint, and this was thrown before the public, as a whaleman throws a hogshead overboard to the deluded whale, which he tries to destroy instead of his real enemy. All these specifications (save the charge of cruel treatment, which she did not make before them, a singular fact if true,) they had gone through with and found *wholly unsustained.* But it was the only rampart of defence which could be thrown up between themselves and the public. This they clothed in the most extravagant manner for the purpose of deceiving the general reader, and this complaint has justly been regarded by all critical minds as a very remarkable legal document. Though almost wholly false, stripped of its verbiage and legal technicalities, it amounts to mere nothing. To show this, I will, item by item, dissect it, and put it in domestic form, still retaining every *charge* and *idea* involved. It has had a general circulation through the public journals ; and those who remember it will know that I do it no injustice by this dissection.

1st. "We were married in Attica, N. Y., the 7th of August, 1856. 2d. Since our marriage we have resided in the State of New York. 3d. He has treated me in the manner the following allegations will show. 4th. He, before marriage

* Edmonds claims to be controlled by the spirits of Bacon and Swedenbourg.

over-estimated to me, as I believe, his social position and financial ability. 5th. He has not practised medicine since our marriage, nor made any attempt to do so, but has devoted his attention to the business of my lecturing, and, therefore, has lived upon my earnings. 6th. I have delivered, in this and other states, various lectures, the proceeds of which he has invested, after supplying our wants and giving me $700. He agreed to supply the wants of my mother, but has given her only $10. 7th. He furnished me with old flannel, of coarser material, for undergarments then I was willing to use, and refused to supply any other but the blanket. He supplied me with expensive and showy outward garments, but refused the flannel. 8th. He has, sometimes, refused to provide me with carriages when I desired; and on several occasions he has neglected to call for food for me after I had been delivering lectures. 9th. He has, sometimes, accepted of invitations to visit our friends instead of engaging board, and remained longer than I deemed it proper for him to do. 10th. He has given me pocket money to supply all my actual wants, but no surplus, only on one occasion, and then only $2. He has counted the number of pieces of clothes given out to the laundress, and has neglected to provide me with a home. He introduced me to two gentlemen (Drs. Folsom and Lions) of his acquaintance, whom I subsequently believed were of a questionable character, but he did not introduce me to any females. 11th. That subsequently to this arbitration he tried to compel me to leave Mr. Wm. A. Ludder's and live somewhere else. He has accosted me in the street since our separation, and used harsh and severe language to me; and he has threatened me with personal violence. He is a large and a strong man, and I am afraid he will inflict some serious injury upon me. He has boasted of his infidelity to his former wife, and of his great powers of seduction. He has been guilty of immoral offences which have damaged my health and delicacy. He has introduced me to a female, and caused me to associate with her, whom I believe is an abandoned character, and he keeps her miniature; and, at other times, he has committed immoralities, and I do not feel it safe to cohabit with him. And for these reasons I wish to absolve the marital relation, and, therefore, petition the court to aid me in my efforts.   CORA L. V. HATCH.

If I have any conception of the meaning of language, I have retained each and every idea in her complaint, and I think that Mrs. Hatch herself, in reading it in its true form, cannot avoid the blush of mortification at its extreme purility. How faithfully she has kept her solemn pledge to me, and her oath before God, I leave for her and the public to decide. No right-minded woman would ever leave her husband on such a basis, were the complaint *true*. This is not all, it is *utterly and entirely false*, from its 4th specification to its close, in all its spirit and nearly all its wording. I made no misrepresentations to her before marriage, for there was no necessity of doing so, and she has repeatedly so acknowledged since. The 5th item as it stands in this synopsis is true ; except I totally deny the earnings being more the result of her labors than mine. The mother's needs I have ever expressed a willingness to supply, and have requested her to draft on me whenever she was in want ; but it is wholly false that it was made any condition of Cora lecturing, or that any such agreement was ever entered into, or any conversation upon the subject was ever held between us. It has been Cora's ambition to lecture, and I have, with great difficulty, restrained her from speaking when she was unfit to do so. And she has frequently persisted in speaking in opposition to my entreaties for her not to. 7th. For more than a year I urged the necessity of her putting on flannel skirts, but she refused, stating that she had never worn them at any period of her life. " The blanket" was of the finest domestic manufacture, and was suggested by me, not on the ground of *economy*, but of *fitness*. When my efforts failed, deeming her unduly exposed, I requested the lady with whom we were stopping, to urge upon her the necessity of warmer clothing beneath her hoops. Without any comment, this lady made Cora two flannel skirts, and requested her to wear them. This is the origin of that much harped-on story, that "her friends were obliged to furnish her with petticoats." It would have been preposterous to the last degree, for me, as a physician, to withhold articles of clothing which could not have exceeded two or three dollars, when her health required it. No rational person can fail to see the absurdity of this item of her complaint ; and her lawyer, who would permit it, ought to be put in petticoats and have a child to lead him. 8th. I have no recollection of ever having denied her a carriage when she wished one, or when it was needful, but, on the contrary, have a great number of times procured them when it was wholly a matter of taste, more than convenience ; and frequently after leaving the carriage she would walk for pleasure much further than she had rode. I have never failed to call for food for her after lectures, when it was not furnished without—even if I had, I see no offence in this, as she could easily ring for the servant herself. 9th. My tarrying with friends was more for her gratification than my own, and while I thank them for their hospitality I regret that she should make her own expressed wishes a basis of complaint.

10th. Our business was such that we were nearly always together, and for this reason she seldom had any use for money, but always all that she required. There was at all times from $20, to $200 at her disposal, in her trunk, to which she was repeatedly requested to help herself whenever in need. Traveling rendered it necessary for us to employ laundresses to whom we were strangers, and when Cora had neglected to count the pieces given out, I have done so, *only* to see that they were returned. Dr. Folsom I have been acquainted with for nine years, and believe him to be a high-minded and worthy gentleman of high attainments. Dr. Lions was a casual acquaintance, of most refined address, who imposed upon me as well as many of the first families of this city. I introduced her, on our arrival in New York, to as highly respectable females as any with whom she has become acquainted since.

11th. I did attempt to remove her from Mr. Ludder's, and to take her to the Astor Place Hotel, which I believed to be a more fit place for her ; but used no other force than to take her by the hand to prevent her from fleeing, and told her that I had come for her. It is *wholly untrue* that I have ever used any harsh expressions to her at any time whatever, or made any threats of personal violence. But, on the contrary, I have uniformly treated her with the greatest possible kindness and forbearance ; and never have had the least inclination of doing otherwise. One singular fact is that, if it be true that I had ever been guilty of any personal abuse, either by word or deed, she did not mention it to the arbitrators. Any threats of personal violence would so have outraged her sensitive nature, that it would have been the paramount specification in her complaint. But during two months of arbitration *no allusion was made to any such thing*. This should be borne in mind, for it is the only important idea contained in her present complaint, and which was inserted by her Attorney to give some show to the matter, though Edmonds is aware it was never made before him.

But duty compels me to more fully explain her charge of " accosting her on the street, and using harsh and severe language." On returning one day from Brooklyn, in Nov. last, I met Mrs. Hatch and Mrs. Ludden in the Fulton ferry-house. I told her that I wished to make a proposition to her, which she could accept or refuse ; but she declined to listen. I urged the necessity of her hearing it. She passed into the street and called for a policeman, whom I informed that she was my wife, and I only wished to speak to her ; and he declined to interfere. After walking together about one block, she consented to listen to what I had to say, (viz.,) " Cora, I am aware of your extreme mediumistic and susceptible nature. You associate only with my most bitter enemies. You absorb their feelings and reflect it back upon me. I most fully believe that if you would leave them, your unkind feelings towards me would soon cease. If you will consent to reside in some family, where they are your warmest friends, and not my enemies, I will pay all your bills, and leave you wholly unmolested ; and then if you wish to separate from me, I will not appear against any proceedings. But believing as I do that you do not realize what you are about, I should feel myself recreant to duty were I to forsake you." She declined the proposition. Here we parted without my having given her an unpleasant word, and I have not seen her since. It was the only time we have ever met on the street since our separation. It is utterly untrue that I ever boasted either " of infidelity to the former wife, or strong seductive powers, or that I have been guilty of any immoral offences towards her." The "female" to whom she has alluded in such disgraceful terms, and whose "miniature" has been in Cora's possession since the day it was received, is a married lady, moving in the first circles of society, and the daughter of one of the first families of our country. Thus, I believe, that I have replied to every idea in her complaint.

These arbitrators are fully committed in my domestic troubles ; and Mapes and Edmonds undoubtedly will continue to do all they can to perpetuate the difficulty. They have taken upon themselves, what I think I may justly say no honorable men would crave.

I have this complaint to make, namely : There were parties under the apparent garb of friendship, who got up the most damning and unprincipled stratagem to ruin my family relations ; and that this plan had been concocted months antecedent to my having any knowledge of it. On my way home from Chicago, the first of Aug., 1858, I stopped over Sunday with a Mr. Sampson in Ypsilanti, Mich., who stated to me that he had recently visited New York, and that he was informed while here that there were efforts being made to separate me and Cora ; and was surprised when I assured him that Cora and I lived in the greatest harmony. In my correspondence with Col. W. A. Danskin, of Baltimore, in which I spoke of my astonishment at Cora's sudden change, he replies as follows :—

BALTIMORE, Aug. 5, 1858.
Dear Doctor:—Yours of yesterday has just been handed me, and with you I deplore the condition of Cora's mind. Your statement in regard to the *suddenness* of her proposition to leave you, somewhat surprises me. At least two months ago I heard that it was said by a gentleman who had just returned from New York, that efforts were being made to separate you, which efforts persons in New York were confident would be successful. I mention this because it may give you some light which you seem not now to have. I heard it without comment, and did not deem it worth while to write you in reference to it. W. A. DANSKIN."

One word more in reference to Edmonds, and I have done with this horrid chapter of iniquity. As a lawyer he declares over his own signature, that the $3,000 we had accumulated by our mutual efforts "*all* by *right* and by *law* belonged to Cora." 1st "By right." I took a girl from poverty, clothed her like a princess, and by untiring toil on my part, and by my financial ability, was enabled to lay by something above expenses. Edmonds had told me that by my management I was doing a greater work for the cause of Spiritualism than any other in the field. Mapes also declared that our success was more the result of my management than her qualifications. And now with a name before the world, she declares her inability to support herself. The labor of those two years was the most arduous of my life, while Cora had nothing to do only about three hours per week to submit to entrancement. Again, full one-third of the $3,000 I made by publishing, was wholly independent of Cora. Notwithstanding all this, Edmonds declares that I "could not control *one dollar* of it without a gross breach of confidence on my part." Wonderful Judge ! ! 2d. "By *law*." I will give the highest authority upon this subject and there leave it.

"*The husband is entitled to the profits of any business conducted by his wife, and is liable for articles bought with his knowledge and assent for the purpose of prosecuting it.*"— *Fourth of Duer.*

But this was conducted by myself.

The matter did not stop here. Mapes had all of my available means (which appears to be a permanent investment, though a part of it is on seven per cent. per annum,) the mortgages being on Illinois property, would not at a forced sale bring one-fourth of their real value. Knowing this, I was pursued with a fiend-like malignity for the purpose of accomplishing my pecuniary ruin ; and Mapes' notes were refused in payment for alimony. RUIN was the aim, and nothing short could satiate this forocity, while at the same time Cora was making $75 or $100 per week, unless she was robbed. Her condition was such that she was ready to sanction with her oath any statement which would subserve immediate purpose. Were I to state all the truth in this matter it would be more libelous than fiction. Byron well expresses the emotions which naturally arise in the soul towards those who would thus ruthlessly trample under foot my conjugal relation, which was far more dearer to me than all things else.

"Oh! wretch, without a tear—without a thought,
Save joy above the ruin thou hast wrought—
The time shall come, nor long remote, when thou
Shalt feel far more than thou inflictest now ;
Feel for thy vile self-loving self in vain,
And turn thee howling in unpitied pain.
May the strong curse of crush'd affections light
Back on thy bosom with reflected blight !
And make thee in thy leprosy of mind
As loathsome to thyself as to mankind !
Till all thy hard heart be calcined into dust,
And thy soul welter in its hideous crust!

Oh, may thy grave be sleepless as the bed,—
The widow'd couch of fire, thou hast spread!
Then, when thou fain wouldst weary heaven with prayer,
Look on thine earthly victims—and despair !
Down to the dust!—and, as thou rott'st away,
Ev'n worms shall perish on thy poisonous clay.
But for the love I bore, and still must bear,
To her thy malice from all ties would tear—
Thy name—thy human name—to every eye
The climax of all scorn should hang on high,
Exalted o'er thy less abhorr'd compeers—
And festering in the infamy of years."

I find in my heart no severe censure for Cora. She is a WOMAN, that is saying the best and the worst. But two years has given me to know that *inherently*, aside from influences brought to bear upon her, she is a *true* woman. She is young, indiscreet, easily flattered and influenced by those she believes to be her friends, and they have thus imposed upon her, and more than all she is a medium. She does not realize that these parties are fighting me through her—that they have secured her youthful confidence without any regard to her real interest, and are willing to effect her ruin as well as mine to accomplish their unhallowed purpose.

Again she was induced to swear in her complaint, that during the sixteen months that I managed the business she made $6,000 or $7,-000—$400 per month. And then when she sues for alimony she again swears that she can make only about $50 per month, notwithstanding the great increase of her audiences in consequence of the excitement growing out of her application for divorce. And on this kind of swearing the court grants her $5 per week. This is not all. Edmonds accused me of having " confiscated her property." I replied that that could not have been a cause of separation, for up to that date it was all invested in her name. She again swears that she " knows of no such transaction," whereas Edmonds *knew* that I had in my possession the original document of a purchase of five acres of land near Chicago for $4,400, signed by " T. P. Abell of the first and Cora L. V. Hatch of the second part" and duly recorded in the county clerk's office. How far Cora knew to what she was swearing I am unable to say.

Her condition is a dangerous one ; sensitive to the last degree, and floating among a most lecherous people. The history of mediums is unfavorable to a hope of a happy termination. I desire her happiness more than my own, but she is not in the road which leads to it. I have sought her relief, but every effort has been contorted into persecution. I know that were she surrounded by a proper religious association and influences she would be brought to see her real condition ; the evil repelled and she redeemed. My request that she should change associations for a while is as little as I can ask. Spirits, as she believes them to be, have, through her own lips, threatened the destruction of her conjugal relation, and her final ruin. The first is brought to pass—time will determine the rest. The Arch Fiend has employed faithful servants for his work of moral destruction. Sad victim of a worse delusion—to suppose the work of devils to be that of angels ! Recreant to her nuptial vows, she petitions the court to release her from the bonds of matrimony, an audacity seldom equalled, and strikes its poisoned arrows at the institution she should uphold. Had she, during my brief absence, acted the part of a prudent wife and avoided her unwarrantable flirtations, promenades, saloon dinners, sherry cobblers, and theatres, she would not have been brought under such influences as to cause her to have entered upon her mad career or sought to absolve her union. I mention this only as it is fit that the cause should be known. One sin leads to another. My enemies thus found her an easy victim ; and the result is before the world. The blow was sudden, and made far more terrible by the happiness which had preceded it.

> " Thou knowest well what once I was to thee ;
> One who for love of one I loved—for thee—
> Would have borne the sins of the world ;
> Who did thy bidding at thy slightest look,
> And had it been to have snatched an angel's crown
> Off her bright brow as she sat singing, throned,
> I would have cut these heart strings that tie down,
> And let my soul have sailed to Heaven, and done it—
> Spite of the thunder and the sacrilege,
> And laid it at thy feet ; but I am as the dog that fondles o'er
> And licks the wounds he dies of."

There is a divine *use* in this separation, whether it be transient or permanent, and that its particulars should be published to the world Our position was a leading one in the field of labor we occupied ; in virtue of which it has already excited more public attention and criticism than all of the multitude of abandonments which have occurred in the Spiritualist ranks. By this means it will become the pivot of a revolution. Many mediums, of both sexes, will be led to see their precarious situation, and fortify themselves against it. The public will be aroused to the reality of the terrible iniquities which are here to be found. It will awaken a general feeling of condemnation, and, finally, blossom out into effectual means of cure. Means are adapted to ends, and I clearly see the hand of God in all this.

As slight, in importance, as this separation may appear to be, future history will prove that it is more than individual. There are a combination of circumstances which escape superficial observation, and which are of more than human planning. Parties occupying prominent positions are engaged in it, and have freely lent their aid, covertly, in breaking down the marriage institution. Perjury has taken the place of manly honor ; deception, falsehood, and fraud, of the deepest hue, have been multiplied without limits. Time will correct all this, and add new proof of the truth of the statements recorded in this work.

In virtue of this, the moral, social and religious bearings of Spiritualism will be made far more apparent than hitherto. The seeming triumphs of its iniquities will prove its own ruin. Its victories will be more disastrous to itself than its defeats. God is victorious over all, and " He maketh the wrath of man to praise Him, and the remainder thereof He restraineth." In Him I trust. Individually, I have gained infinitely more than I have lost. Launched as I was upon the broad ocean of pantheistic philosophy, without chart or compass, and no reliable pilot at the helm ; the stern rocky coast of materialism enveloped in fogs ; unseen islands and whirlpools of ruin surrounding me on every side, while the tropical tidal-waves were rapidly bearing me on to the coast inhabited by moral cannibals ; I cannot but feel to rejoice at my escape, by whatever means. Thus situated, and opiated into religious indifference by false theories, no less affliction would have aroused me to consciousness. I fostered an idol in my bosom until it arrived to maturity, it received nourishment and strength from me until it became powerful, and then, like the magician's rod, demons transformed it into a serpent, and with its poisoned and forked tongue of slander, it turned and pierced me to the heart. But God only permitted the poison to arouse the latent energies of the soul, and then substituted the Balm of Life.

> " I will not complain, and though chill'd is affection,
>   With me no corroding resentment shall live;
> My bosom is calm'd with the simple reflection,
>   I have done you no wrong, you have naught to forgive.

CHAPTER III.

PRACTICAL WORKINGS OF SPIRITUALISM.

The Spiritualists of this country are divided into two distinct classes.

1st. The *Christian Spiritualists*, or those who believe in the phenomenon of Spiritual intercourse, but regard it not only wholly unreliable in its teachings, but also to a very large degree disorderly and demoniacal in its bearings and influence. This class deplore the opening of an intercourse with what they believe to be the hells. They hold that mediums are often demoniacally obsessed as in the days of Christ; that there is an *Infernal Influence* from the nether regions which is improving any and every opportunity to deceive mankind, subvert their judgment and insidiously inculcate into the minds of all who are susceptible or credulous the most corrupt and demoralizing doctrines and practices, until they bring them into the most intimate relation with all that is evil, and in this way accomplish their ruin both morally and spiritually. This class take the name of "Christian" in virtue of their belief in the Divinity of Christ; and they believe the Bible to be a Divinely Inspired Revelation from God, and containing an internal, spiritual meaning, or significance which only the spiritually enlightened can comprehend. They are nearly allied in their faith to the Swedenborgians. Of their uprightness of conduct I have seen nothing which demands criticism. They are few in number and unobtrusive in their association with the world. They believe marriage to be a religious institution and of Divine order, and as such should be perpetuated through life. Here we leave them.

2d. The *Harmonialists*, under which head may be classed three-fourths of the Spiritualists of this country. They take their name from a belief in the Omnipotency of God as an all-pervading and permeating principle, and the Inspiration of every faculty of the human mind; and that " all seeming discord is but harmony not understood;" evil has no positive existence as such, and its apparent manifestations are only the outworkings of those conditions which God has implanted in the soul, and which are needful for the individual, and are only preliminaries to a higher condition; there is no retrogression, but eternal progress is the motto upon their gospel banner. The men and women who are the most deeply steeped in vice and iniquity are equally on the highway to Heaven as the self-sacrificing apostle of Jesus, for if these conditions exist it becomes necessary that they should be out-wrought and thus spend their force, and in this way work their own purification. To these the Bible is wholly rejected as authority ; it is a history of wars, vices and superstitions ; and though it may be of use to ignorant people, it is transcended by the "Harmonial Philosophy." Progression with them is a fixed principle. The wave of the ocean is constantly forward, as much say they, when in its trough as in its swell, white and crown-capped aspiring to the sky. As is the progress of individuals so is that of the history of the world. Therefore, the nineteenth century is capable of higher inspiration than the first.

I am not controverting but simply stating this philosophy. It will be understood that I am giving their theories and some of my observations of their practical workings, and leave the intelligent public to decide for itself.

Aside from these two classes, there is a large number who cannot strictly be classified with either party, but who believe in the phenomena of Spiritual intercourse, but retain the belief of the churches of which they are members, or from which they have just emerged. These are those who give character and stability to the cause. They are men and women who take a rational and practical view of life, and are quite disgusted with the extreme and fanatical class.

There are great fundamental laws pertaining to mind, well established in both Europe and America, which more fully explain and show to us the awful danger of one mind being held in subjection to another, whether the controlling mind be in or out of the external form. By following out these laws we shall find the key to unlock the mysteries of the immense amount of evil among Spiritualists, which now so shocks and disgraces the world. I do not intend to be severe but only to relate facts which are the legitimate result of conditions not understood why mediums become so perverse both in theory and practice. In a former chapter I have given my idea of the class of spirits which control or obsess minds on earth, and move physical substances. Now imagine one of these demons, though he may once have been an inhabitant of this earth, to have control of any mind, arch, shrewd, and cunning to the last degree, and who wishes to accomplish, not in a day, but finally, the greatest evil to mankind, and Spiritualism is that. They are precisely like devils on earth, only more shrewd and patient. Evil men do not show their real character until they have created conditions to accomplish their object, friendship is first established, then destruction. I have had a bitter trial in this school of devilism ; and I do not think that they will need any lessons to make some of them successful operators even in hell. Pleasing doctrines are no more evidence of good spirits than is apparent friendship and flattery, of those who covertly seek our ruin. In both cases the motive is the same. Here lies the difficulty of persuading Spiritualists of their awful danger. Most, like myself, will be taught alone in the school of experience. A greater number will become themselves demonized, and lost even to a desire for good.

Psychology has well established the fact, that one mind may be held in perfect vassalage or subjugation to another—speaking their thoughts and echoing their emotions. In other words, there is some force exerted, directly or indirectly, by a human being, which flows in or is received and yielded to by another. In virtue of this law, the wildest hallucinations and most insane ideas may be made to appear as realities to the subjugated mind. The magnetiser, even at the midnight hour, may inform his subject that before him is a beautiful variegated rainbow, and upon the centre of its arch is perched an eagle ; or that his cravat is a coiling anaconda, ready to strangulate him, and to him they become realities. No human testimony, outside of the *will* of the operator, can dissuade him of the reality of the hallucination. He simply *knows* that he is correct, and all testimony which does not come from the magnetiser utterly fails to reach his understanding. This law is well understood by millions who do not believe in spiritual intercourse.

All Spiritualists claim that the mental control of mediums is *spiritual psychology*, and that for the time being, the mind of the medium is held in perfect vassalage to the controlling spirit. Also, that the spirit-world is made up of just such persons as are daily passing from this world to that, and that both the good and evil alike have power to return and obsess mortals who are mediumistic. Therefore, taking the concession of the Spiritualist, and combining it with the well known laws of psychological control, and we are inevitably forced to the following conclusion, viz., that there is no reliance to be placed upon the veracity, or moral integrity of any mental medium on earth. Their oath would be wholly unreliable, for the moment they are called upon to bear witness they may become infested or obsessed by an outside influence, which desires to give different testimony, and thereby made to utter such statements as they know to be wholly false when in their normal condition ; and at the same time they may be, apparently, perfectly themselves in reference to all other things. Here we have a basis, according to the Spiritualist's own theory, which is incontrovertible, and which establishes upon immutable laws the perfect unreliability of mediums.

I deem this to be an important point, and crave the indulgence of the reader while I give two or three instances in illustration of this idea. 1st. While I was a student in a Medical College in Cincinnati, I attended a course of psychological lectures. In the audience was a Methodist minister, who was most bitterly and enthusiastically opposed to the doctrine of Universalism. He proved to be a psychological subject, and by the will of the operator was brought upon the stand. He not only renounced Methodism, and caricatured it in the most severe manner, but advocated Universalism as the only doctrine of the Bible. When relieved, he became very indignant with the man who had placed him in such an awkward position.

2d. Soon after marriage to my present wife, one day she was entranced, in the presence of myself, Dr. Knapp and lady, at that time residents of this city ; a ring was placed upon her finger by the entrancing power, accompanied by the pledge that she should not externally know of its existence. She wore the ring for seven days, and while apparently perfectly normal to all other things, she had no ability to discover the presence of that ring, even when her attention was directed to it ; and it was only by the united testimony of her husband and friends, that she was induced to believe that it had ever been in contact with her finger. She would have readily, and conscientiously sworn before any magistrate that she never saw said ring.

Mr. Sunderland, while giving public exhibitions of psychology in this city, obtained control of a Mr. B., who was among his audience, and drew him upon the platform, and presented him with a piece of white paper, declaring it to be a check of Mr. B.'s own drawing on the bank where he deposited his money, and that on the following day he should present it, and draw five hundred dollars. He then withdrew his influence in all respects, save the check. Thus, while Mr. B. was perfectly normal in every other respect, he presented his blank paper at the appointed time to the bank, and demanded his five hundred dollars, and became very indignant when informed that his supposed check was only blank paper. He resolutely affirmed that the check was of his own drawing, and was real. In the dispute his delusion passed, or, in other words, the influence was withdrawn, and Mr. B. was greatly mortified to see the awkward mistake he had made. I give these examples which clearly prove that a psychological subject (and all mediums are such) may, as in the case of Cora, state things wholly false, and at the same time be irresponsible. It was on this basis also, that I found an excuse for Edmonds.

I have entered the arena as a champion against the iniquities which are so universal in disorderly spiritualism, and which I most solemnly believe to be the greatest enemy of God, morals and religion that ever found a resting place on earth—the most seductive, hence most dangerous form of sensualism which ever cursed a nation, age or people. I cannot write the whole truth without laying myself liable to prosecution for publishing obscene articles ; and aside from this objection, I could not so offend public taste ; therefore, the reader must only expect some of the milder forms of the heinous realities which here prevail. They establish themselves behind the rampart of what they technically term the " sovereignty of the individual," and hold themselves responsible neither to society or God. Thus fortified in their theology, they make free to worship the god within them, whatever it may be. On marriage the Spiritualists are peculiarly eloquent and emphatic, as it strikes at the foundation of all well regulated society. They are divided into several classes upon this subject.

1st. Those who believe in the oneness of marriage—that there is somewhere in God's universe a true conjugal partner for each individual, with whom they are to live forever. That with this partner, even notwithstanding all the imperfections of human nature, there would be unalloyed bliss. If any discord, or any lack of their highest idea of love creeps into the domestic relation, it becomes evident that they are not truly married, and are living in adulterous relations with another individual's partner. Upon this basis it becomes expedient that this relation should be absolved, and a new one formed with some fortunate " affinity" which some officious spirit-guide has had the wisdom to designate. Discord again creeps in, and they soon conclude that both they and the spirits have made another mistake, and, not in the least discouraged, they try again, and so on until their moral and social condition becomes offensive to every honorable and virtuous member of society. A large number who believe in this theory, in consequence of their domestic condition or social relations, do not carry it into practice, but give their hearty approval to all who do. This doctrine is freely advocated both by spiritual lecturers and papers. The *Spiritual Age* says :—

"The truth is, that the existing marriage institution, or at least the prevalent marriage customs, are fearfully corrupt and false to man's higher nature. Where true marriage exists, alienation, desertion and crime are impossible."

In this view of the subject, all who in any way prove infidel to their marriage vows are perfectly justifiable, as the wrong itself becomes positive evidence that the parties are not " truly married," and consequently under no obligation to each other. In other words, this is a philosophy which proves to their minds that social corruption and conjugal infidelity is no wrong, but a fidelity to their higher or interior nature.

Again I quote from a communication to the *Spiritual Telegraph*, bearing date January 1, 1859. This is in reference to a lecture delivered by Miss Dods to the Spiritualists in Clinton Hall, Brooklyn :

"She argued that the present law regarding marriage and divorce was oppressive and wrong, should be repealed, and a law enacted authorizing either party, when they were abused, unhappy and led a miserable life, to appear before some appointed officer of the government and be allowed an order for a divorce ; that the parties should have the same legal right to thus divorce each other that they had to be married at their own request—divorce expenses being thus saved.

After the lecture a warm discussion ensued, which resulted in admitting the ingenuity, soundness and eloquence of the lecturer. It was certainly an original and noble effort, and ought to be published."

It appears by the writer's own statement that these sentiments, after being duly discussed, were approved by the audience. I ask, who can fail to see that it is an entire and perfect abrogation of the marriage institution, thus leaving individuals to change partners every day if the pleasures of their lascivious desires shall so require ? I am not unjust in quoting their own language, and I firmly believe that the above quoted paragraphs will find a hearty response from a large majority of the Spiritualists of America ; and some of the most noted among us have given their individual sanction to this condition of things. Thus, I confirm what I previously stated that this class " is popularizing those social conditions which every good citizen must most deeply deplore."

The marriage institution lays at the foundation of all well regulated society; and unquestionably is the most sacred, holy and divine relation which exists among mortals or angels. It should be entered into with a full conviction of adaptation and use; and when the relation is once formed, nothing should ever be allowed to mar its beauty and harmony. What the parties are not to each other, it becomes their duty, in virtue of their relation, to try to develope. It cannot be denied that the history of mankind has most clearly shown that the happiness of the domestic relation has depended upon the estimation or sacredness in which this institution was held. The ratio of domestic discord and unhappiness is as the freedom and ease of procuring divorce. I, therefore, question whether any high-minded and discreet person can desire any greater leniency in our laws regulating marriage in this country than now exists. Let Indians, which in this respect must ever stand as a reproach to our nation, receive all the profligate and renegade men and women who desire to absolve their nuptial relations for their own wrongs or offences, but let New York maintain her dignity.

2d. There is another class of Spiritualists who believe that every faculty of the human mind, being implanted by Deity, is capable of direct inspiration from Him; therefore, that every inherent desire should be gratified in the way of its promptings. This, to them, is rendering obedience to the promptings of the Divinity within them, and thus becomes a religious duty. They aver that the ultimate of love is promiscuous, and is curtailed only by arbitrary and unwholesome regulation of society. To usurp their freedom, to them becomes a moral obligation. Monogamic marriage is thus made an outrage against the promptings and inspirations of the god within them—that the relation of the sexes is not so much a matter of delicacy as a fastidious and perverted society would make it appear. The most of this class claim to act upon the principle of policy, and refrain from publicly promulgating their sentiments and practices, as they believe that the world is not yet sufficiently advanced to receive their doctrines. Some aver that all true love seeks the happiness of the loved, and is unselfish in its nature; therefore, if the husband or wife can find pleasure in the arms of another, it becomes their pleasure to have them so do. There are those who are prominent and active in the promulgation of the spiritual philosophy who most fully endorse this sentiment. It may have one thing to commend, viz: it destroys all basis of jealousy. This class believe true virtue is fidelity to their desires. One of them, writing to the *Spiritual Telegraph* in reference to an unmarried woman who had just become a mother, uses the following language:—

"It is reserved for this our day, under the inspiration of the Spirit world, for a quiet, equable, retiring woman to rise up in the dignity of her womanhood and declare in the face of her oppressors and a scowling world, I will be free! God helping me, though I stand all alone, penniless, friendless, homeless, forsaken of all—I will exercise that dearest of all rights, the holiest and most sacred of all Heaven's gifts—the right of maternity—in the way which to me seemeth right; and no man, nor set of men, no church, no State, shall withhold from me the realization of that purest of all aspirations inherent in every true woman, the right to re-beget myself when, and by whom, and under such circumstances, as to me seem fit and best."

Here we have the theory and practice combined, which the editor of that paper most ably controverts. But I believe it is the only spiritual paper in America which would do so. The same writer above quoted further adds :—

"Our spirit friends say, all purely natural passions must have ample scope to work themselves out in their true order. The hoops which have bound the past must be burst, and narrow conventionalism must be disregarded; legalism, so far as it fetters the body or highest aspirations of the mind, must be trampled under foot, and a high and holy freedom must take their places."

Can any one ask for a broader basis of prostitution than is embodied in this sentiment? What would be the condition of society were all "developed up (downward) to the same standard?" The marriage institution is here held in open contempt, and "should be trampled under foot," and that, too, by the dictation of spirits. Maidens are recommended to usurp their rights and ask for lascivious indulgence, and when the sacrifice of their virtue—the crowning excellence of woman, which sits like a coronet upon her brow, all adorned with the diamonds of purity—shall cause her to bring forth the fruits of her sin, she is then unblushingly to say it is my God-given "right to re-beget myself when, and by whom, and under such circumstances as to me seem fit and best." With my feeble perception and "undeveloped condition," I must confess that, to me, no other social sacrilege equals this. Nevertheless, there are men in this city, who possess high social positions, in virtue of their wealth and intelligence, who are so infatuated by this doctrine that they freely offer their own daughters to become the mistresses of men ; they aver that marriage should not precede, but follow that intimate association which belongs to husband and wife ; that after they have lived together sufficiently long to ascertain whether each can fully respond to all the desires of the other, is then the proper time to decide on marriage. The only real difference between this and the other class of Spiritualists is in the *time* of marriage ; for the others believe that the nuptial relation should be absolved as soon as the parties find that they are not fully adapted to each other. The experiment of adaptation, beforehand, has the merit of saving the expense and trouble of divorce. With either class, marriage is shorn of its sacredness and becomes a mere co-partnership, to be nullified at the will of either party.

I should deem it an insult to the judgment of the public, to point out the terrible consequences were these doctrines to generally prevail—the poverty and wretchedness from the want of wholesome family regulations ; the destruction of both physical and mental powers ; the multitude of children of unknown fathers ; the illegitimacy of all hereditary property, and the universal chaos and confusion which would everywhere ensue. Go where we will among the Spiritualists, and we find conjugal harmony and fidelity the exceptions, and not the rule. There are mediums who possess all the education and charms of highly accomplished ladies, who believe it to be their

God-appointed mission to break up the conjugal relation, and for this purpose they pass from house to house, and claim the husband as their "affinity," until the ruin of the family is accomplished, and then pass on to another.

Profane and intemperate men, libertines, adulterers and adulteresses, are openly upheld and encouraged by the Spiritualist societies all over the country, as their public teachers in their sacrilegious worship. Women, thirty or forty years of age, with children growing up around them, and who have abandoned their husbands, of whom they were not worthy, and who are living in adultery with their paramours, produce abortion, and arise from their guilty couches and stand before large audiences as the medium for angels. It is freely acknowledged in their public journals that moral character is no test of qualification for a public teacher. Private circles form no small share of this evil and delusion ; these are formed by placing a man by the side of each woman, and all joining hands. The affectional and emotional feelings are actively exercised, and the magnetic force of the entire circle becomes concentrated upon the most beautiful and susceptible female members, and the result may easily be conjectured. The magnetism and lust of the circle upon the susceptible members, are taken to be the control and dictation of spirits, and, therefore, rendering submission becomes a religious duty. There are, also, those who are called "Developing Mediums," claiming that they are the appointed agents through whom the Divine inflatus flows for the development of "passional attraction" in females—that all functions are rendered healthy and vigorous only through *exercise;* and that the fastidiousness which prevails among those ladies who do not believe in promiscuous concubinage, arises from a lack of physical and spiritual development.

The healing mediums come in for their share of the plunder, and resort to every species of fraud and deception to accomplish their hellish purpose. The horrors which here exist are too outrageous for utterance, and I must pass them over in silence, farther than to say that their new method of imparting their spiritual magnetic force has, in nine months afterwards, given fearful "cries" of its efficacy. The internal plan of conjugal love, of most mediums of both sexes, becomes perverted, and it appears impossible for them to maintain more than a sense-union in their nuptial relations, and there is a perpetual tendency to form extra-marital and libidinous associations. The brutilazation of many of them become so great that virtue and truthfulness, as a real fact in moral consciousness, become nearly unknown. Their lust rules in the centre of their will, and their bodies become energized as they become the seats of enormous appetites of demons.

The Bible, Christianity, and with a large number even virtue, veracity and common honesty are thrown overboard by this hell-infested and God-forsaken people. Husbands inviting men to occupy the beds of their wives ; wives soliciting of other women indulgences for their husbands. Rape is rare, as it implies an unwillingness in one party. But bigamy, abandonment, adultery, fornication, thefts, perjury, unmitigated falsehoods and slander, and direct efforts to break up family relations, and to destroy the marriage institution, are everywhere rife among them. Sodomy, with parties conniving in the crime, and then "black mailing," was recently perpetrated by one of the most prominent mediums, and then hustled out of town by other prominent Spiritualists to escape the penalty of their crime. They are constantly crying "progress," which only appears to be in the direction of iniquity. They subvert all human dignity and public morals, and destroy all we hold most dear and cherish most sacredly. Spiritualism is a masked and hideous monster, with no heart, no conscience, no real intellect—for its philosophy is baseless—but all passion and emotion. It leaves the soul without chart or compass or rudder, to run upon every rock, and into every whirlpool of ruin, where they will all bring up, sooner or later, who do not return to their senses. France, in its days of infidelity, or Sodom and Gomorrah, never presented a more diabolical bedlam than the Spiritual associations. No unprejudiced mind can for a moment critically investigate the condition of this class of people, without being driven to the inevitable conclusion that the curse of God is upon them, and that moral, social, and pecuniary ruin are almost inevitable to its victims. I thank my God, far more than for any other event of my life, that I have escaped from among them.

My task is ended. I dedicate to the world my observations, of a portion of the results of that Spiritualism, which I can most truly say has been the bane of my life. I hope that, in the providence of God, I shall be permitted to retire from any further action in this cause; and seek my happiness in fields more prolific in fruits of Peace and Righteousness. With such an experience, is it strange that I have awakened to the awful horrors and terrible realities of an intercourse with unseen beings, and flee from their influence, and warn others against like misfortunes? or in "giving heed to seducing spirits and doctrines of devils : speaking lies in hypocricy, having their consciences seared with a hot iron ; forbidding to marry." 1 Timothy 11 : 2, 3—and thereby more effectually open wide the flood-gates of iniquity, and cause the polluted streams of lust and an inverted moral condition to overwhelm mankind. To all who yield to its influence its FINAL will be damnation.